THE LONELY COMMUNIST MAN

THE LONELY COMMUNIST MAN

Thuyen Huy

iUniverse, Inc.
New York Bloomington

THE LONELY COMMUNIST MAN

iUniverse books may be ordered through booksellers or by contacting:

iUniverse
1663 Liberty Drive
Bloomington, IN 47403
www.iuniverse.com
1-800-Authors (1-800-288-4677)

ISBN: 978-1-4401-4597-1 (pbk)
ISBN: 978-1-4401-4596-4 (ebk)

Printed in the United States of America

iUniverse rev. date: 5/26/2009

For
All friends who were imprisoned in the concentration camp 15NV of the Vietnamese Communist Regime in mid 1975 after the fall of Saigon

Chapter One

Dropping the hoe down on the narrow dike which divided the exhausted rice field of about two hectares, leased from a landowner at Tram Vang village since the day their first child, Bon, had been born who was now just five years old, the sun was burning in middle of the day although there always were plenty of wind on the field, Lay stopped working and pulled the ragged T-shirt up to wipe the sweat off his face, then sat flat on the ground next to the row of aged custard-apple trees. Lay opened the small sheath of areca tree, grapping a handful of cold boiled rice and eating hastily in order to be able to have enough time finishing the crack part of the field before the rain coming.

There was only two third of the unfertilised rice field could be used, the block which Lay and his wife tried to save cent by cent after many hard working years, since the beginning of their marriage in Dau Tieng village then they came to Tra Cao hamlet, leased it with a low yearly payment in hoping that they will have a better life one day. Five years had already gone by, their limbs, hands, feets had become callous; from the early dawn to the late night they still had not enough to feed three persons. Bon, their innocent boy drank boiling rice slop day in day out instead of milk. In a poor crop year, even the land-owner had pity to make the repayment lower the debt was still as at the beginning, they tried to ask for delaying the repayment date many times. Bup, his wife, endured her plight in silence to toil and moil all day and night in helping her husband, Lay loved his wife's bad-luck destiny who was married to a pariah man, has been weather-beaten without a word of moaning. The knowledge had just filled up about a square of his hand which has been over-learned from people, Lay was parentless in early day, tending water-buffalos at the age of five but he had always tried to teach his boy to learn the alphabet as much as he could in dreaming that his boy, Bon, would be able to go to village school one day.

End of the rice harvest season, his crop was down once again, he still could not afford to pay the debt of last year they took their boy, catching the ricked passenger coach to Tram Vang village to beg the landowner once again allowing them to defer the debt until next year. Standing to wait for the coach on the roadside, Bup took few remaining Dong (Vietnamese dollar) in the pocket of her ragging South Vietnamese pyjama to buy a half of a yesterday bread roll with few pieces of salmon and tomato sauce for Bon, she was pleased to hug her son then they sat on the kerb of the black tar road in the middle of the district market, letting people comes and goes. Bon swallowed his saliva and chewing the bread appetizingly in the baking sun evening.

From the rice field, Lay came back home with the bamboo basket and few tiny anabas, Bon bustled in and out to meet his father. He gave him a dark blue Paradise fish, the sole and only toy that Bon had. The column of grey smoke of dinner cooking rose slowly over a couple of spattered thatching houses far away in the deserted field. Here houses in the hamlet were apart at least a few dikes. At night, looking at the boy sleeping on the tearing cotton hammock, the broken thatching roof, the bamboo curtain that did not cover the door fully, the sound of his wife's sigh as the sound of bull-frogs in cold and rainy nights, Lay had his heart rent and tossing about the whole night.

Off the passenger-coach at the main gate of the Cao-Dai Central Temple, Lay carried the rush-bag leading the way, Bup hold the boy's arms behind they went straight away to the office of the administrator of the orphanage. Bon naively ran up and down on the shining and colourful tile floor. The couple had tears in their eyes and felt deep grief to sign the consent paper for giving their boy away. The old administrator was not be able to hold back his feeling, took the glasses off to wipe his tears off. Bon followed them to the playing hall being happy when seeing other boys of the same age playing noisily, he did not hesitate to rush in and joined the crowd at once and letting his poor parents sobbed their hearts out. They stayed at the orphanage until the dinner time, said goodbye to the administrator then left there quietly. Bon did not notice anything, continued playing in the loud sound of the laughing. Bup cried like a mourner at a funeral on the way back to Go Dau Ha town, Lay bitted the trim of his old cotton hat, felt his heart tearing in pieces.

The rainy season came, the Lays plot was deserted, grasses were not cut and weeds grew up to the knees. The thatching hut with the broken roof seemed to collapse so did the coco leaf curtain which stroke back and forth when it was winding. The row of the chlorotic Malabar nightshade lay quietly next to the ricked and worn wooden bridge. Lay was not there any more, not long after the day when villagers started to plough their fields. The couple with a few ragged bags and few hundred Dong, returned the land to the landowner, left Tra Cao hamlet in a pouring rain day. The row of custard-apple trees were full of fruits which has just began to ripe next to the row of sad seed-bananas trees, Bup pulled the piece of plastic cover that was picked up from a fertilise bag somewhere, saved it as a rain-coat, covered hastily over her head. Lay walked not far behind, letting the rain poured down on the muddy and slippery dikes.

The sky was cloudy and pretty dark. The sun seemed to set down earlier. Sitting on the wooden chair under the front veranda, in the yard, the fence was obscured by the row of mango trees, if the metal gate was not opened wide, Mr Nhan could not see people and all sort of vehicles moving up and down to the market. The isolated villa has became desolate gradually, sometimes Mr Nhan who was a primary school principal once in the time of the French colonised government then the Diem regime, people in this city always called him "Mr Principal" although he retired long time ago, wanted to talk to his wife, Mrs

Nhan, who was genial, kind-hearted and always helped her neighbours whenever they needed, about adopting a child. Mr Nhan and Mrs Nhan had three children, the two elder sons were studied in France then stayed there, the last daughter has married with a rich businessman in Long Xuyen province who has just come home once a year in the Lunar New Year festival (Tet). Going up and down in the house, it was desolate everywhere, some days they did not feel to touch the dinner. They used to sit there looking out the quiet front yard while the sun set slowly over the river.

After the Tet festival, Mr and Mrs Nhan dropped by at the orphanage on the way back home from the Tri Hue Cung temple, they met the administrator looking for a child. Bon was now six years old who wandered about dumbly alone in the yard and kept his look down at them. Suddenly they felt to have a pity on him and agreed that he was nice and cute so they talked to the administrator. The administrator called Bon come over, asked him to stand next to them. Bon crossed his arms and bowed down to greet them, the Administrator recalled Bon's story. Mrs Nhan caressed his hair, touched his hands, Bon smiled with rounded lips. Mr and Mrs Nhan came back to the orphanage a couple of times afterward and deciding to adopt Bon as their adopted son.

On Saturday morning, Mrs Nhan woke up very early, packed a new set of clothes which she had just bought from the market few days earlier carefully and a box of French biscuit that still had the smell of butter into a big carrying bag. She made a hot cup of dark tea, sat next to the window waiting for the morning. Mr Nhan also could not sleep well and got out of the bed a moment after his wife. The Myrna bird stretched its soaking wings on the stone steps in the yard next to the old foot of an ochna tree that was till in full of yellow flowers although the Tet festival (New Year) was over. The cup of tea was just cool down, vehicles began to pour noisily on the streets, Mr Nhan grabbed the wool hat and put hastily on his head, Mrs Nhan adjusted her scarf round her neck then closing the gate. Gradually night dew had disappeared at the end of the street. There already were a few sun-rays.

Bon was dressed in too loose new clothes, he carried the box of biscuit in arms running up and down and was busy to talk non-stoppable to his friends then he came to greet the administrator and an old lady who looked after them with a round arms and a low bow. They all stood to wait outside. Slowly Mr and Mrs Nhan walked out. Bon was not far behind, sometimes looking back. There was no one in the playing hall, even one.

The light was now still on in the midnight, Bon could read and write the alphabet and knew the multiple table by heart not long after being in this house, he asked to be taken with Mr and Mrs Nhan whenever they went, greeting Mr Nhan's friends and other people politely with a bow. Entering the first year of primary school, the teacher let him be promoted to higher class although it was just half academic year, every one showed their respect as an excellent pupil. Bon was easy to teach and passionate to read and doing home-works. Bon often hung around Mr Nhan in helping him to root out the weeds, swept the dead leaves in the garden all year round. Every afternoon they stood in front of the gate waiting Bon went back home while the dismissal bell rang over the yard of the provincial primary school.

Chapter Two

From Dong Co hamlet Lay and his wife came back to the orphanage to look for their child. One informed them that Bon had been adopted by a family in town not long since they had left. The administrator gave them Mr Nhan's address. They took the paper and caught a motorcycle-cab to Tay Ninh town.

Lay stood with a halt at front gate a while then hitting to call, Bup was quiet behind her husband. Being sitting under the shade of a mango tree at the corner of the back yard, Bon ran to the front gate when hearing the strike. Bon bowed low to greet them then walking back into the house.

-Mother, we have visitors!

Mrs Nhan pulled the robe straight down and put her glasses back on then following Bon to walk out. Lay and his wife stood still at the same spot, the two opened their eyes widely looking at Bon without a blink. Seeing the strangers, Mrs Nhan was afraid of their mistakes so she asked them slowly:

-Who do you wish to look for?

Taking the paper in her husband's hand off, Bup stammered:

-Is this Mr Nhan's house?

Mrs Nhan nodded and asked Bon opened the gate wider:

-I am Mrs Nhan, what is the matter… alright please come in, we will talk about it over inside.

Mrs Nhan turned back, Bon ran before her and stood waiting on the stone steps at front door, Lay and his wife stooped timidly behind. Mr Nhan stepped out and invited them to enter the lounge room. Mrs Nhan went to the kitchen. Bon helped her to bring some teas then walking out with a reading book in his hand. Mr Nhan repeated his wife's question:

- What do both of you want me to do?

Lay drew the consent of giving a child paper out of his pocket, handing to Mr Nhan, tears ran down his face, Lay talked about their poverty, they loved their son who they did not want to see him to be suffered as they have so at the end they had to give their child away while there was no other choice. Bup also sobbed her heart out. Listening to the story, Mr Nhan and Mrs Nhan were moved and could not say a word. Mrs Nhan called Bon coming inside, he stood next to Mr Nhan's chair, looked at them in turn. Lay stopped talking and looked up Bon opened his eyes round. Mrs Nhan hold his hands, pulled him toward her, she looked at Bup with sympathy:

Bon is your blood child anyway indeed. She turned

to Bon, pointed her finger to Lay with a shaky voice, she went on:

-Bon! These people are your blood parents, let greet them now.

Bon did not understand a thing but rounded his arms and nodded his head:

-Dear Dad and Mum.

The call of "Dad and Mum" made Mr Nhan had tears streaming in his eyes. Lay and his wife sat still without a word and cried. They desperately wanted to hug their son but were reluctant to stop. Mr Nhan stood up quietly and looked at his wife:

-Well, we will leave you a while so you can talk to Bon, if you need some things just let us know.

Mrs Nhan followed her husband, caressed Bon's head:

-Just stay with your parents, be a good boy!

A long moment after, they were back in the lounge room, Bon was sitting quietly on the chair, Mr Nhan asked him to go out, Bon once again rounded his arms before walking away, suddenly Bup told him:

-Be careful, do not let you fall!

-What will you decide now? Mr Nhan held his glasses and looked at the couple.

Bup spoke up with a soft voice:

-Because of the poverty, we had no other choice than to be resigned ourself to give our child away, we had our hearts broken, we felt ourself as a guilty person but we hoped one day we would be better in order to take him back. We asked for your pity and begged you to allow us to bring Bon home, your nurture and foster in the past years, we would never forget and please accepted our prostrates.

Lay and his wife kneed down on the floor, bended half of their bodies down to prostrate Mr and Mrs Nhan. Mrs Nhan quickly held them up.

Mr Nhan took his glasses off:

-In three years, we are very happy to have Bon in this house, he is a good boy and very intelligent but he is your child anyhow, you have tried to be here looking for him, we are speechless, we will surely be so sad and lonesome if he will not be here anymore. As you know, we love Bon very much but we can not do anything now....well at the end he is your child we hand him back to you....

Mr Nhan stopped talking a moment, wiped the stream of tears running down on his face, Mrs Nhan added:

Would both of you make your mind easy, we would not dispute this matter, Bon would understand what is going on, I hope that you would let him go to the school after taking him home as he is very keen to study.

Lay and Bup stood up and cried very loud without a word.

Mrs Nhan handed to Bup a new plastic carry bag that was full of clothes, shoes and books. Bon wept aloud, it made Mr and Mrs Nhan also wept, Mrs Nhan handed to Bup few hundred Dong (Vietnamese dollar) as Bon's gift. They walked Lay and his wife to the gate, Mr Nhan held Bon in his arms, just told him that they would come to see him in a next few days. The motorcycle-cab was disappeared at the end of Vo Tanh street but Mr and Mrs Nhan did not go back into the house. It was scorching sun in the midday.

In early winter, gently the autumnal cold breeze blowed, the dead leaves covered most of corners of the back garden, it was a long time no body swept it. Bon had gone, The Nhan's has saddened so much, the house seemed to be more desolater than when there was not Bon here, Mrs Nhan stopped firing the leaves in the yard in early morning and looked at the morning cold dew alone. In late afternoon, Mr Nhan had his heart wrung with pain when listening to the class dismissal bell on but the heavy metal gate was not opened. Bon's classmates yelled Bon's name out in the street when they passed by sorrowfully. They had not wanted to talk about the adoption again as they were afraid of that situation. Mrs Nhan tasted a few drops of hot tea gently, looked at the misty view outside, it was a foggy morning, she suddenly felt a cold has just touched her heart and thought about Bon if he was cold somewhere. The gate of The Nhan's villa had been rarely opened since the following winter days.

Chapter Three

Dong Co hamlet lay desolate in the middle of a vast rice field and parched thatch in scorching summer days along the highway to Saigon city. The foot-path that led to the highway from the head of the hamlet was about a kilometre long. It was covered full of dust in this dry season. Housing, most of them were made by thatch and mud except those brick one which were hamlet government offices and the hamlet primary school. They were next to each other but not on the straight row. A military post lay on this side of the highway, its piles of barbed wire looked like a spider web and covering by a lot of worn sand bags around. Outside the army post few muddy puddles were steeped in water that had been stagnated since last harvest. The watching militia man sat alone in the small watching tower who looked at the passenger coaches went up and down on the highway which stopped dropping the hamlet people off sometimes did not say a word, just nodded his head with a cool smile. Farther from the end of the hamlet, the waste high hill stretched out to a small creek banks that had been covered only half of water-level all year round. Few old trees stood up to defy the bake sun, a couple of rice-straw huts where a band of buffalo boys hung round talking gossips while waiting their cattle chewed the dried grasses wearily on the vast field where it was always green despite it was rainy months or sunny days.

The Lay's family came to Dong Co hamlet from Tra Cao village with all the money they saved after long and hard working days and the money that had been offered by the orphanage when they left their child. They bought a small block of land on the hillside at the end of the hamlet. They built a tiny thatch house and worked for other land-owners in the surrounding area as labourers. When the fishing season came they went catching river fishes then walking to the Binh Nguyen market about four kilometres from here to sell it. Their lives were still not better and still in straitened situation.

In a couple of first days after being back to Dong Co, Bon wept softly for a long time while thinking of Mr and Mrs Nhan, Bup loved and took pity on her boy, she tried to comfort him. She took him to the tottering and only candy stall of the hamlet, next to the fence of the hamlet primary school and bought for him some old biscuits and sweet that begun to smell because of the scorching sun. Bon pulled his mother's hand to point to the row of classes when passing the school, the pupils' sound of reading aloud made Bon so gloomily sad. Bup said no word Bon got used to it gradually afterward, two days then six days, there was no Mr and Mrs Nhan's news, he was disheartened and joined with the boys of next houses to play while waiting to go to school as he had been told.

Some days before the Tet festival, Mr and Mrs Nhan caught the coach to Binh Nguyen town in early morning they brought with them a lot of candy, cakes and new clothes which they have bought in Tay Ninh market few days earlier. They asked people on the highway the direction to Dong Co hamlet. Getting off the coach, luckily they were guided by a militia man in the post at once they walked deliberately to the centre of the hamlet. Bup was sitting to weaver the bamboo basket in the front veranda was surprise and bashful when seeing them. Bup invited them going into the house and walked to the back yard to call her husband home who was helping someone to build up a buffalo stable. She poured some fresh water into two broken cups then placed them on a tottering wooden table and cowered before them. Lay and his wife stood next to the other side of the table, midday wind swept through the house that had only a few pieces of thatch wall.

Looking around there was no boy's sign, Mr Nhan started to ask:

-Well, does Bon go to school?

Lay kept quiet, Bup tried to smile:

-No, he might play somewhere. Let me go to take him home. She had just put the palm-leaf hat on head and walked out hastily. Mrs Nhan looked out. Bup went to the vast field at the end of the hamlet.

Lay sat on a section of an old tree trunk that was used

as a stool and was looking up to Mr Nhan and stammered badly:

- Bon goes to tend the buffalos on the field from the dawn.

Mr and Mrs Nhan sat motionless, looked each other to shake their head:

-My God, that is not right!

Tears were welling in Lay's eyes, he cried:

-We are too poor and being driven to extremity, how will we do?

Bon followed behind his mother to go into the house, bowed low to greet them, his face was pulled long down and almost cried. His clothes were torn into separated pieces. His hairs still had the sun smell and became the burnt colour. Mr and Mrs Nhan had their hearts rent at his appearance, Mrs Nhan held him in her arms, repeating two words of "pity" over and over.

They had not stayed there long, left all the goods that they bought with them behind to go home sadly. Lay and his wife walked with them to the highway and so did Bon. Standing to look at the coach that disappeared gradually over rice fields, Bon suddenly was aware that he would never see Mr and Mrs Nhan again, Bon wept in secret and whispered "mum and dad". His cry was vanished in the evening cold breeze.

The war started after these days, the Viet Cong (Communist guerrillas) who flickered to wait the night falling down, from Duc Hoa, Duc Hue areas came to attack Dong Co militia post few times. There were already a few villagers who joined the Viet Cong forces. Dogs barked loud around at night, sometimes the hamlet government office was burnt down, the flame was flaring up brightly. On the highway, at the section between Go Dau and Trang Bang district, mines were exploded sometimes, a couple of man were dead. The band of buffalo boys had not stayed late on the fields, it was just late afternoon they were hurry to take their cattle back to the hamlet, there was no more chance to sit down to talk about their landowners, the rivers or the girls who once bathed in the creek while looking at the sunset over the river.

The new harvest season begun, there were few uncultivated fields this year especially those in the other side of the creek that was along the Vam Co Dong river. At night the Viet Cong guerrillas waited for South Viet Nam Militia forces were back inside their base then mixed secretly to each house of the hamlet to threat villagers and collected rice tax. The South Viet Nam men indeed did not dare to come out to far unless they had reinforced forces from the district military headquarter. It often rains this time, usually in the evening when the sun was mostly setting. Bon rounded up the cattle, took them back to the landowner. He yelled out to let them know that he was already back. Bon took the clothing pack that was hidden under the pile of rice straw at the back of the house the day before and walked hastily up to the moor. Again Bon looked back the wavering light of the kerosene lamp in his house once more time then wiped his face. Bon walked on in the silence. A few night storks flew sluggish over the end of the moor, Bon left Dong Co hamlet at the middle of the grow rice season when he was just eleven years old.

Chapter Four

Luong, the Viet Cong platoon leader of Binh Nguyen area, with a cigarette on hand who sat quiet in a secret rice-straw hut on the other side of the muddy foot-path that ran in the middle of the dark moor. Next to the mouth of a tunnel, he calmly looked at Bon who was having a bath in a narrow creek. Under the cover of leafly and virgin forest where they had just stopped for a while to wait for the nightfall in order to take Bon crossing the river to Boi Loi Viet Cong secret zone. Here they could avoid the watching of South Viet Nam forces L19 plane that carried out the spy mission from the air. Waiting for Bon finished his bath, Luong handed to him two balls of press cooked rice with some mixing peanuts and salt which was the ration of the guerrilla dinner as usual. Bon took them and ate straight away without a word. Bon carried his belonging creeping into the tunnel after emptying the last piece of rice in his hand. The cold night wind had just come,

Bon shuddered with cold and lied down trying to sleep as at midnight he would follow these Viet Cong men to use the small barges to cross Vam Co Dong river.

In comparing with other boys of the Viet Cong revolutionary martyrs, Bon was the most educated one. That is why he was elected to be the leader of the Uncle Ho Chi Minh youth team of Boi Loi secret zone. Here in first begining days, Bon was really in home-sick particularly Mr and Mrs Nhan, the more he thought of them the more he was terrified by his plight of buffalo tending boy during all years in Dong Co hamlet but afterward Bon got used to be with his new life. Bon joined his group joyfully, to practise swimming cross the river, to creep into the dark tunnel when their position was bombed by the South Viet Nam forces A 37 jets. Bon was keen to learn the communism ideology, to debate the aim of the revolution which seeks to destroy the unjust, the oppression and the liberation of South Viet Nam as uncle Ho Chi Minh has guided. Bon studied carefully and properly each uncle Ho Chi Minh's single word as his superiors had done so, not because he understood deeply these ideas or dreamt to be a leader like uncle Ho as his friend but Bon was just keen to read, a full page of words of a book, the front page of a yesterday newspaper, all made him more exciting whenever seeing them, it did not matter what these words meant. Bon followed his group sometimes to move in the night to attack the South Viet Nam posts in some hamlets in this area in order to gain the practical experiences of the battle.

The Viet Cong provincial company leader appraised Bon's achievement in the role of the Boi Loi youth team leader who also proposed Bon to be selected to participate in the Uncle Ho Youth general congress that would be held in the R-zone in Mo Vet area, the Front of Liberation South Viet Nam's central secret zone that was built as their safe haven inside Kampuchea land, along Tay Ninh provincial border. There would be the central delegates of the Communist Party come to join them from Ha Noi, the capital of North Viet Nam. On the departing day, Luong, the platoon leader accompanied Bon to Tra Cu hamlet, from there another liaison man of Long Giang platoon took over. The South Viet Nam provincial forces which joined with the National Navy launched an operation to comb the vast rice fields area in the villages of Long Khanh, Long Chu right at the time Bon arrived. Bon had to stop there and stayed in the tunnel in a couple of days. The South Viet Nam forces overran the area and destroyed a number of Viet Cong local bases. The Viet Cong platoons had dozen death men. At the end, after few days with the dinner ration of sweet potatoes Bon had just arrived in Mo Vet on the opening day on time. Roads in the R-zone were shadowed by communist flags and banners. Boats and ships had come and gone in a rush. There were a huge crowd of men and women around the rows of military barracks and stores. Men in communist uniforms rushed up and down, it was too noisy as the district market day. Once again Bon was also selected to represent for the South to read the speech which extolled uncle Ho services, promised to study and work hard to be worthy of being good nephew of Uncle Ho. Bon, on behalf of all youth members of the South, made an oath to the fatherland's south iron bulwark. Bon imitated to repeat what his leaders had said, exactly what the Viet Cong cadres were taught from the top leaders down to the bottom one.

After the general congress, Bon stayed at the R-zone then followed one high committee member of the Front of Liberation of South Viet Nam who also was the Central Communist Party member in Ha Noi to go to the North before the Provisional Revolution Government of South Viet Nam was formed in order to continue his study of general education and political theory. Bon followed the communist logistic regiment to the three border area of Kampuchea, Laos and Viet Nam in the central highland of the South made their way up to the North on Truong Son foot-path. Early season rain poured down over each leaf, each tree and their heads. The Truong Son virgin forest was too glacial during his trip. The central committee member who held a ministerial position of the Provisional revolution Government of South Viet Nam later on was a graduate of law from Paris, France and practised as a lawyer in few first beginning years of the Ngo Dinh Diem regime (the Republic of South Viet Nam) but being dissatisfied with this government afterward. He opposed this regime then joined the Viet Cong secretly, left Saigon with the dream of the liberation of South Viet Nam that was launched by the Ha Noi communist men. There he thought of his family sometimes, he thought of his son who was in the same Bon's age. Considering Bon who was active and intelligent, he asked Communist party to allow him to adopt Bon as an adopted child. He sometimes used fake identification of South Viet Nam people to be back secretly in Saigon city trying to see his children but did not dare to stay there long as the South Viet Nam police and security forces had been so tough.

In Ha Noi, the two lived lonely in a lot brick house at

the end of the street to Ho Tay (the West Lake) which was granted by the Ho Chi Minh regime when he married again with his second wife who was from Ha Dong province and was a manager of a bicycle factory. They lived together in four or five years, she then had a lung cancer and died after one long fighting year. He stayed widowing. At home he tried to teach Bon to learn the French language, the foreign language that he spoke fluently as his native Vietnamese language. It was not long Bon read and wrote properly. His foster father was very satisfied in hoping that one day when the South would be liberated, the child would continue his dream on the revolutionary ways.

Graduating from high school as an outstanding student who had a deep understanding of communism ideals and the policy of the Party, Bon was approved to be a communist party member then was granted to study abroad in Moscow in order to obtain modern knowledge of Marxist-Leninist and practical means of communist system on the world. Bon was appraised as an example for the youth over the North on the party newspapers, Bon as the favourite son of the revolution. They asked all students have to study Bon's case in every school from primary to high schools and from hamlets, villages to towns and cities in many continuous years. The foster father was proud of his adopted son and smiled all year round although he and his son were still in poor living standard.

It was pretty glacial, the whole city was covered in the morning mist and gloomy as a horrified cemetery. Bon left Ha Noi in an early winter day on the old commercial plane of big-brother Russian.

CHAPTER FIVE

End of the spring, April 30th, the battle of the liberation of the South Viet Nam was ended, Republic of South Viet Nam was defeated, last President of South Viet Nam ordered his men to surrender. The Northern Communist Forces, men and vehicles noisily marched into Sai Gon city which had been renamed as Ho Chi Minh city as soon as the red and yellow star flag was hoisted on the flag pole of the Municipal building. Bon was not a real stranger in this crowded city which was always noisy and animated even though the Communist Party called it as a city under the oppression, because Bon at least had lived and carried out underground activities here in nearly a year. Back home from Moscow, Bon was provided a different personal history and necessary fake documents from the Party then moved secretly to Sai Gon city to be employed as a worker in the Vinatexco textile factory in the outskirt of Sai Gon. Bon rent a small house in Lang Cha Ca quarter and from here Bon set up a propaganda section that recruited new members in working class people and labourers. Those days, although Bon had already seized the communism ideas in his mind but sometimes sat on the kerb of crowded streets, he seemed to have to recognise that here the living even under the domination and oppression of the South Viet Nam puppet regime was still happier and richer than Moscow city where uncle Ho and the Party called it as a heaven of communist men. After one year, Bon handed over this position to other cadre who entered Sai Gon from the R-zone, returned to Ha Noi. It was not long after Bon got married with Linh, a girl who also studied in the same class in the cold Moscow city.

Having been in the South and Sai Gon city, one had to agree that Ha Noi was very poor. The Northerners all tried to go to the South cheerfully and brought with them what they have saved in almost twenty hard working years in thinking that it would help their relatives who had still stayed back in the South but they could not believed to become the beggars in this rich city where they called a perfect heaven in their dreams. Bon moved into a pretty villa on Doan Thi Diem street, with a few policemen, its owner was an army general of the South Viet Nam forces who left Sai Gon two days before the city was taken, a narrow and quiet street with two green tree lines on both roadsides. In the house, everything was untouched and even clothes that was intact. A couple of children bikes and a Honda motor-bike sat against the garage wall, the lawn of the front yard were still green and fresh. There still were few pieces of red fire-cracker of the Tet festival remaining on top of the bush of night lady- flower at the corner of the back yard.

Bon was a powerful man in this city although no one could find his name on the list of the Ho Chi Minh military administration committee. Beside the position of Chief of the Party Ideology Bureau Bon was the Chief of Political Executive section. The Third Group that was a political left-wing in Sai Gon before 1975 or writers and journalists who could not leave Viet Nam all were terrified when being invited to this office. There were not many people who knew his face except a few senior cadres of the city party committee and police department. Bon was engrossed in his duties, he loves the communism ideology. He has always dreamt of the equal society without oppression and exploitation. His works devoted only for the Party and by the Party. He trusted his communist party and he absolutely believed that what Uncle Ho said was always right. Bon was proud to be a communist man who served for the cause of Uncle Ho services.

On the way back to Tay Ninh city, Bon stopped by Dong Co hamlet looking for his parents, Lay and Bup. The South Viet Nam militia post next to the highway was not here any more. A lot of new houses had been built up since, rice fields was still scattered. Old trees on the top of a high hill where Bon sat protected from the sun while watching the buffalos eating grasses had not been changed but it looked so withered than before. His driver stopped the Russian made jeep at front of the hamlet office, Bon walked toward his old thatch house that was now covered firmly by all the mud-walls. The owner said sorry when Bon asked where about his parents. There was no one of his old buffalo-boys group.

In the night that Bon left Dong Co, Lay and his wife were panic-stricken to go to search at the section of the river that was next to the rice high fields with a crowd of villagers who thought that he was drowned. It rains in buckets and pretty dark, they gave up after two days. Lay and his wife then caught the passenger-coach to Tay Ninh looking for Bon in hoping that he might be at Mr Nhan's house. They were slightly ashamed not dare to go inside and stood still at the front gate, Mrs Nhan was also not pleased to invite them coming in while being told of that news. Mrs Nhan sobered without a word. It was not long after returning Dong Co hamlet, Lay sold the house and the block of land then leaving there for Chau Doc town in the delta of Mekong river. They had not been heard since that day.

It had just been noon Bon arrived Tay Ninh city, Mrs Nhan who was sweeping dead leaves in the front yard stepped out to have a look while hearing a car was stopping at the gate. Mrs Nhan stood motionless and had not yet to recognise the man in a communist uniform, Bon called "mum" gently and opened the gate wider keeping way for his jeep. Mrs Nhan embraced him firmly in her arms. Tears were streaming down on her face. She turned to walk back:

-Mr Nhan, Mr Nhan! She calls her husband's name.

Bon led her by his hand to step up the stone steps, the driver carried a couple of bags slowly behind. Mr Nhan has just walked toward the door, Bon held his hands:

-Father, here Bon is, this is Bon!

He had not been able yet to said a word, Mrs Nhan pulled Bon toward her side

-Mr Nhan, this is Bon, this is really Bon! She was in melancholy.

Mr Nhan had tears bursting out his eyes, took his pair of glasses off and leaned on Bon's shoulders walking back in. Three persons sat looking each other happily and sadly in silence. Bon's driver took the belongings to the back room. Bon recalled his story slowly from the pouring night when he left Dong Co to the days when he joined the Viet Cong guerrillas, entered the R-zone then went to Ha Noi, Moscow and in the end he came to Sai Gon under the flag of the Liberation Front. He was proud to tell them that he was now a communist man. Mr and Mrs Nhan had compassion for his life that was suffered a lot but they also looked each other quietly and thought "that was over" when listening the three words "the communist man" from Bon. That dinner, there was not much things to take, just a couple of bundles of steamed water morning glory and a bowl of boiling black bean. It was long time Mrs Nhan did not often go to the market. Her youngest daughter who lived in Long Xuyen city left Viet Nam with her husband on a merchant ship on April 30th 1975 was living in Nice southern of France. The two tossed about sleeplessly all through the night. In the recent campaign of elimination of the capitalist class that was ordered by the Communist Party, although Mr Nhan was retired long time ago who was called to report to the new provincial people government a couple of times. That was not included a band of communist cadres who came to Mr Nhan's villa to ask the owner's documents right at the day their forces took over Tay Ninh city. He was fed up with the Chairman's tedious lecture that has been repeated days in days out. Mr Nhan has been told that he was a lackey for the capitalism and French colonialism which dominated children's mind, he carried out the American and the puppet regime of South Viet Nam policies to teach the Southerners being against their revolution, he was a rich man with a big house and land while the people were sucked out of their last drop of blood. Mr Nhan bursted out laughing when listening to the Provincial communist chairman emphasised the words of puppet and colonialism as he clearly knew what he wanted. Few days before, he had come and pretended to visit Mr Nhan's place, he tried to have a chat with them and looked around the house.

Bon woke up very early, his driver went to the kitchen making a cup of tea then stepping out to check the military jeep. Bon followed him walking around the yard and the corner of the garden. Bon seemed to be pleased to show him where he often sat to read the reading book under the shade of the old tree, where he set all dead leaves on fire in the winter days, Bon smiled regretfully. Mrs Nhan made a couple of low drying cough, Bon carried his cup of tea coming back in the house and sat on a wooden chair next to her. Mrs Nhan tasted the tea gently looking at him:

-Are you so busy, why do not stay here few more days?

Bon put the cup on the table and nodded:

-The government is just been received, there are a lot of tasks to be done in making sure that everything will be alright, besides we still have so many enemies which are till plotting to topple our achievement. That is why I have to go back to work, ah mother!

Mr Nhan had just walked into the room when Bon ended his talk. He stood at front of the altar which was in the middle of the room. He looked up his parents' photos and said softly:

-We will not know that how long you will be back to see us once again, we are afraid that we would not be here at that time.

Bon was so surprised to look at them, Mrs Nhan saddened to shake her head, Bon made a slip of his tongue:

-Any matters, or you plan to sell this house?

-It is still lucky if the house will be sold easily! Mrs Nhan replied tiredly.

Mr Nhan then talked to Bon the story of the Provincial People Committee and the Chairman's attempt to confiscate this villa and shook his head:

-We now have no choice, Bon ah, the policies of the party is implied the same everywhere.

Bon stood up and said nothing, he ordered his driver preparing the jeep, tried to make his clothes little even then walking out. Before stepping in the jeep Bon looked back and said to them:

-I go to the city for a while!

Bon had gone, they did not look out. The gate was left opened wide. Bon returned home in late afternoon. He handed to Mr Nhan a pile of documents and asked them to keep it in a safe place. Bon left Tay Ninh in that early evening. Few days later, the Chairman come to Mr Nhan's place again but he had asked them politely and gently to ignore what he had done and accepted his apologies. The next wave of inventory of assets, there was no communist cadre came to Mr and Mrs Nhan's as before.

Chapter Six

Bon returned to Ha Noi to see his godfather who was a minister of the Revolutionary Government of South Viet Nam which was declared a death without clarinets and drums after the Communist Party proclaimed the unification of the North and the South. He was now very sick and frail without a cent in the pocket. His living was relied on the small pension payment from the government every three months including the ration of rice, meat and other needs. Fortunately he still had the house, if not, he had lived on the street long time ago, however he still kept the hope that his Party would make this country ten times richer than before as uncle Ho said. Bon was told about this hope although there was often no rice left in the plastic bucket sometimes and the electrical lamp was on only a couple of days in a week. Linh, Bon's wife, brought to him all the gifts which they bought from the

South and left few thousand Dongs (Vietnamese dollar) for him just in case before they went back to Sai Gon.

The campaign of detaining officials and military personnel of the former south-Vietnam government who stayed behind in concentration camps was succeeded perfectly. On the other hand, the hunt for the capitalists, the religious leaders, the intellectuals and the artists or journalists who have once opposed the communist ideology of the North government in the South during the last twenty years had still secretly gone on. The prison Pham Dang Luu and the prison Chi Hoa were crowded of the said-reactionaries who needed to be re-educated. Bon was utterly dedicated to select the detainees with the support of the Southern new-communist man whom the Sai Gon people called them as the April 30th gangs. Bon gave orders to arrest any one who was considered as a danger for the people on the way to build a proletarian dictatorship of the communist government.

The one was said as The Military Administration Committee was disbanded, the entire administration system of the South at this time was reorganised exactly the model of the North structure. The sign of City People Committee was erected on the top of the old municipal building, North soldiers were not seen many in the streets but the policemen in tan uniforms overflew in this city. Linh, Bon's wife who now was the manager of Vinatexco textile factory had her own driver and a couple of servants.

It started to have some bribery affairs in SaiGon, one tried to run about soliciting favours, to bribe senior cadres of the City party committee for the early release of their relatives who were imprisoned in Long Giao, Dau Giay,

Nha Trang, Moc Hoa or Ka Tum concentration camps. The Sai Gon people began to talk of new kind of business, there were some one were really released. The payment was paid by piece of gold, not the money note. The gold flea markets were set up around Le Thanh Ton street and next to the Indian pagoda. Those markets were very bustling. Policemen often kept quiet in return to receive the bribe. It was not long after almost policemen of the Ho Chi Minh city had new Honda motorbikes instead of the bicycle made from China. The Sai Gon people relied on that chance to live in the friend-relationship of comradely feeling with communist officials. Whoever had a close connection with some powerful cadres who were on high position such as army general, tried to offer them every thing, televisions, motorbikes, cars, refrigerators, and even money in asking them to say some things for their relatives. Those generals, chairman, managers politely accepted these free gifts but the prisoners were still in their camps after waiting days long. If someone came to ask about it, the briber has just smiled gently saying that let them be re-educated few more months in order to be a good citizen. It was not only a few senior cadres but it seemed that the whole Ho Chi Minh city officials were on the same boat.

The campaign of abolition of the comprador bourgeoisie class in Tay Ninh had just been over. Some of Mr Nhan's friend properties were seized and confiscated mostly except their only own houses where they were living. Their lives were never like before, there were no more cars, nor more Honda which was now belongs to the revolutionary men or belongs to the people as the new regime called it. The most luxury Toyota cars in this city now had been owned by the Chairman, the Secretary who was on behalf of the people to use them in serving for the people. It was still lucky whoever showed any objection and trying to oppose their orders would be deported to Bu Dang, Cay Xieng, the new economic zone where there were only wasted land and virgin forest. In this time, Mr Nhan and Mrs Nhan were aware of the fortunate would not come twice sooner or later, they took the advantage to use all documents that Bon has left. They put the villa for sale and moved to a Tay Ninh suburb after buying a small block of land with a dozen of mangos trees, grapefruit trees and a timber house at the three-ways cross-road in Giang Tan town, next to the highway. Few months later, Mrs Nhan once went to the town market and passed her old villa by a chance, she realised that The Chairman of the Provincial People Committee was living there. Mr Nhan decided not to let Bon know about this matter and regarding Bon was no longer in their family after the day they returned to Tay Ninh from Dong Co hamlet more than ten years before.

Tram stood waiting for Linh right at the Manager's office door after the lunch time. It was a fine rain, there was no worker gathering in the back yard of the textile factory as usual. There now were not many of her old worker-mates left. Those had just came from Ha Noi who were so nice but not able to be close friends while they had different thinking and ideal. Mr Duc, the former chief of engineering section left Viet Nam on April 29th night with his family, the communist government took over the textile factory, Tram missed her boat, stayed back. The new administration board asked her to be on Mr Duc's position until today. She hoped to be replaced one day but a few years passed but there was still no word at all. Tram and her husband, Man who was still employed by the new education department as math teacher in Vo Thi Sau high school tried to escape few times but unsuccessful. It was really easy to work with Linh who was polite and gentle and had a little well-educated than the others although she was also a communist. She had sometimes joked with her subordinates and workers despite they were the Southerners or Northerners. She has always smiled to greet all people around. As the Chief of Engineering section Tram met Linh almost everyday so she got used to it, the two girls sometimes had lunches together and talking a lot of stories, the story of formerly when the war was still on and the current affairs.

The afternoon shift leader who stepped out from Linh's office seeing Tram had greeted her with a smile and walked away hastily. Linh invited her come in. The two sat next to each other on the row of chairs against the wall, it was really sunny outside. Looking at Tram Linh asked joyfully:

-Have you had your lunch yet?

Tram answered with a fresh smile:

-What about you, will you not go home today?

-There are few things I have to finish today urgently moreover I am not feeling hungry. Well if there are some works you need to do I leave you alone to go back to the factory building, Tram had just both said and stoop up.

-No, that is alright, just a couple of daily reports, please stay, any thing I can help you?

Tram sat down:

-I like asking you to do me a favour, but it is after

you, if you consider that it is easy to help, if not, please ease yourself.

Linh was excited in laugh:

-What is it about so tense, please let me know, I will do it right away in my capacity.

Tram started to recall the story with a melancholy voice, she asked Linh to say few words with her husband to permit her uncle who was a retired army colonel of the former South Vietnamese government since 1960 and was the principal of the blind infant school was imprisoning in Day Giay concentration camp. Although being almost blind, he asked his children to take him to represent the Ho Chi Minh city authority when the order was announced on radio. He had been taken to Day Giay camp not long after. He was now seventy years old and had a serious liver ulcer. It seemed his life was nearly over. His family had made a lot of petitions to the city government, from this office to the other but they had no responses.

Tram had her tears ran down and sobbed:

-It is pity for him, if he has a chance to die at home, that is enough happy for my family so I beg you as a friend, please help us, I will never forget this gratitude in my life.

Linh looked at her and nodded:

-I promise to talk about this with Bon to see any thing he can do in this circumstance but this is still depended on the party authority, Tram ah!

Tram felt easier in her heart, she had spoken out what she want to talk at least. Tram held Linh's hands saying thank you then leaving. Linh stool still to look her walking down to the hall of the central building.

Sunday morning, few following days, it was very early, the midnight dew had not yet melt in the streets, Tram and her cousin sisters who were her uncle's children caught the coach to Long Khanh city, they brought Bon and the City Party committee's letter of authorisation with them which addressed to the Director of Dau Giay camp. It has not noon yet when they arrived at the camp, the director had gone to the morning market. They sat waiting in the guest huts outside the fence of the camp, not far from the main gate. It was quite quiet in the camp, a couple of policemen walked up and down without a word, few thin and sick prisoners sat weary under old trees at a distance away who were allowed not to go outside to work. The healthy men had been taken with the Northern soldiers going to cut trees in deep forest since the dawn.

The camp director read the letter several times, looking at Tram's group one by one, he seemed to be in deep thinking. He took time to drink his cup of morning tea while trying to ask a few nonsense questions in a pure Northerner accents. He called the guard in, said some things with a very low voice then waiting for the guard stepped out. It began to be baked sun in the sand yard. Tram and her sisters sat motionless seeing her uncle who was tired, quite haggard carrying the rag-bag leaned on the guard's shoulder walking into the office. They have bitten their own lips and shredded in tears. The Director touched her uncle's shoulders, said nothing. He took out the order of release from the draw of the desk, handing it to Tram. His children held their father's arms to support him standing still up. Tram opened the bag and placed two boxes of moon cakes, some jars of Chinese tea on the camp director's desk as few more day, it would be the mid-autumn festival. They said thank him with sob voices then stepped out the office hastily as if the director would change his mind. On the way to three-crossing road where they would catch the coach back to Sai Gon, they held him firmly and cried aloud. In their dim curtain of tears, the concentration camp began to be smaller gradually over the virgin and dark forest.

In the afternoon, Tram and her sister rode the bikes to Bon's place as promised. Linh greeted them at the front gate, the female servant was watering the flowers in the front yard, looking up to say hello and waited for them came inside to close the gate. Tram carefully put the gift box which was packed properly on the side table that stood next to the lounge then said thank them for helping. Suddenly Bon was touched, the emotion that was similar with the one he had when coming back to Tay Ninh to see Mr and Mrs Nhan again after many long years. Bon looked at the gift box then around the house, what the former army general of South Government left behind was still as it was before, Bon had not bought any thing even they wanted so. Luckily they could save thirty or fifty dong from their monthly salaries. Sometimes Bon realised that around him, even Linh who had the same thought, from the quarter, the districts to the city officials and cadres seemed to be richer than before, they bought brand new cars, brand new houses and had party all time. The Chairman's house, the Party Secretary's house were renovated with a swimming pool and Chinese garden, no one wanted to keep the old Russian jeep which was only used in the Truong Son trail in the anti-American war days. Their wives and children had gone shopping from early dawn to late night. Bon tried to ask himself and answered for himself when sitting alone in his office. In the old days when the South had not been yet liberated, in the North, although the government was very stable for a long time but the corruption, the bribe still occurred in the senior and top cadres of the government and the party daily besides Saigon was a rich city so it was not hard to understand this situation. Bon considered this matter as the man's mistakes. It was not the policy of the Communist party. The Party was always lucid and they still had the law, whoever was guilty would be judged and punished fairly. During the time when they had just won the war, there were not many bribers, corruption cadres but in the recent years that number was increased ten-folds but there were just a few to be put in jail. This matter made Bon's thought was landed in an impasse however he had still believed his party, his lessons of Marxist-Leninist which he was educated in order to serve the people as uncle Ho words. The couple were reluctant to accept the gift. Bon left the house not long after receiving a phone call. The female servant took the bike and rode off to somewhere a little while ago. Ha, Tram's sister stood up and walked out to the yard. Tram took a small package out from her carrying bag and hesitated to look at Linh:

-Another thing, also this is a small present for you, while Bon is not here.

She stopped talking a moment, opened the package, five bright gold bars on her hand, she handed them to Linh and said:

-This is a present from my family's heart, I know that will make you will be difficult to accept it but in our friendship, please take this in order to make my uncle happy before his days coming as you are always our saver.

Linh stood transfixed at the offer to look those gold bars. She had never seen them indeed in her life before. Linh was puzzle saying word by word:

-Oh! No, I can not take it, Tram! I will be in deep trouble if Bon know this affair, the other box is alright but this is not.

Tram wanted Linh to understand that her superiors were in big corruption, five gold bars did not matter, but Tram tried to entreat her:

-At this time, you and Bon may need in case sometimes, if Linh refused to take it I will not dare to report to my uncle, maybe he will be upset more than I think. Please.

Linh kept in silence, her eyes were opened wide. Tram put the gold bars into her hand:

-Let take it, there were only you and me to know this happening, keep it in case.

Ha walked back in the lounge room, Tram stood up quickly and looked at Linh without a word so did Linh. Linh walked them to the gate, after riding the bikes at a distance they looked back, the gate was still opened wide.

Chapter Seven

End of the autumn, there still were few thin autumnal cold breeze although it had already been early winter in Sai Gon. This weather was nothing in comparing with the numbly cold of Ha Noi. Bon and his wife sat in silence. They did not want to have dinner tonight although it was being dark outside after returning home from their old friend who was the 5th district secretary on Hong Bang road. Huu was in the same class with Bon when they were in high school and was now a rich man and wore all new western suits. He did not bother to throw away all old fashion clothes in the corner of the back yard after few years. Bon, in contrary, was still in the communist cadres' uniforms, the Nam Dinh white khaki shirt and the dark green cotton pants all year round. He had a new Peugeot car instead of the Russian jeep. Bon's wife, Linh had a close friendship with Tram so she was able to know the living way of Sai Gon people and her people who were holding all high positions in the machinery of the government in the South but it seemed to Linh that she and her husband gradually became the minority group in the prosperous of Sai Gon today. Bon felt dispirited when reading all reports of his men who accused all normal people as the reactionaries cynically. Linh stood up and walking into the kitchen, just took few bowls and pair of chopsticks, Bon followed behind then they sitting down to have a late dinner in the dark corner. Bon thought of what Huu had said to him once: "in this situation, the politic was not important than economy".

The South had been in the fit of fever of escape, at home or in the streets, everyone talked about the escape, a few underground groups that organised to smuggle people out of this country were in good business, there were a great number of people who had escaped successfully from the coast line but also there were a lot people who were caught too. Inmates from concentration camp were released gradually however they all tried to go days after. The Ho Chi Minh Party Committee held many internal meeting to look for a measure to prevent this matter, police force was ordered to hunt and arrest these people at all cost day and night. Criminal prisons now received in addition another kind of prisoner including infant without exception. The Government seized more vacant houses in Ho Chi Minh city, the senior cadres ignored their comradely feeling to vie with each other in taking properties, the lower one tried to dispute every pieces of gold.

Friday evening, after work, Tram and her husband went to see an old friend who was a literature teacher at

Suong Nguyet Anh girl high school before. He now ran a liberation book shop on Nguyen Trai street. His family had organised a small party to celebrate their father, a former army major of the South Viet Nam force, who had just been freed from Moc Hoa prison. At the dinner, he ate a little, asked every one a lot of questions of the past few years. On the day he was taken to the prison, Tram and also her friend's family thought that it would be long time if their father would be released however Tram's friend tried to run about soliciting favours, luckily he was in right path. When seeing Tram and her husband off, he let them know that a Chinese Vietnamese friend, tycoon Ly Luong Tan's nephew helped through Huu, the Chairman of the 5th district to pay 12 gold bars and he added that it seemed Mr Huu shared these gold bars with the Chief of Political Executive Bureau, not only him, Tram looked at her husband, both of them thought of Bon right away but kept quiet on the way home.

Sai Gon was in the heavy rain, it had stopped in a couple of days. Leaves had fallen down in rags and covered over the public gardens and streets. Linh looked out the yard of the factory through her office window. The car park was totally deserted. Morning shift workers had left since early morning. Over the road, a row of houses were alternate lay with some flood rice fields which made her to think of Ha Noi suddenly, a sorrowful homesick, she had missed the morning dew of the end of winter days in the narrow streets of Ha Noi city but Linh has not yet come back there. Sai Gon was a miracle city where the Northerners who once had arrived, they all had lingered to stay even one more day in order to have their dreams coming true, seeing Sai Gon once was enough in their life, there was nothing else to regret. Tram shouldered her carrying bag, walked along the hall going home, she had just knocked Linh's office door gently as it was still opened, Linh looked up:

-Have you gone home yet?

Tram walked in, stood next to the desk:

-It is still raining so I need not to be hurry.

Linh tried to ask Tram staying a while:

-So just stay a while, we will have a chat, there are still few things to do but it is not so urgent, I will do it tomorrow.

Tram took a chair then sat down next to Linh, the story at her friend's place yesterday was still hung in her mind, Linh wanted intentionally to know a little more about:

-Will you go back to Ha Noi in the Tet festival of this year?

-It will not, Tram ah! my father planned to see us in Sai Gon this Tet. Besides Bon also want him to go to Sai Gon at least once.

Tram smiled:

-So you have to prepare now, if your father will be here for the Tet, you have to spend some more money obviously, if you need some thing, do not hesitate to ask me, ok?

Linh sighed softy:

-As you knew we have got that much money, our monthly salary is just enough for us to live, if my father coming, we have to save more before he will be here. We felt pity for him who has devoted his whole life for the revolution in more than thirty years at the end he had nothing.

Tram tried to add:

-Because you do not pay attention on this matter, there are a lot of cadres who had held lower positions than your husband, but they spend a lot on new houses, new cars, new things, they all were being rich quickly.

Linh was totally quiet. Tram talked about twelve gold bars which her friend had bribed, Huu, the Chairman of 5th District, also Bon's friend. Tram had pretended to know nothing:

-Do your husband know Mr Huu, he seemed to be very rich.

Linh nodded, Tram went on to recall the story of the bribe and the share of gold bars. Face had changed the colour. Linh had been amazed looking at Tram:

-Is this true, to be honest I did not know any thing, perhaps Bon did not do such thing, you are our closest friend who could understand our situation.

Tram held her hands to talk softly:

-I said nothing against you, but I am afraid that Huu will take advantage of your husband's name to harm Bon later on.

It had just stopped the rain outside. The evening sun had just risen. In the front yard there were a couple of late sun-rays, Tram stopped her talk at that moment, Linh took her handbag and walked with Tram to the car park. Before turning to the way to her car while the driver was waiting, Linh turned to Tram said gently:

-Thank you for let me know the story, I will talk to Bon about it.

A few female workers went home late who pushed the bikes passing them nodded the head. Tram stood still to look out until Linh's car disappeared over the fence of the factory. The rain balloons were broken one by one on the larger cement yard. Over the Tham Luong bridge, a few blocks of dark cloud had still hung above the row of trees on both side of the highway.

Chapter Eight

Tram intended to wait for Linh at the front of the office but the noisy voices from inside made her to decide walking away. Just few steps, suddenly the office door opened, a few men in army uniforms stepped out with their carrying cases. Tram stepped aside making ways and slowly nodded her head to salute as they were all strangers. In the hesitation, Tram stopped thinking to go to see Linh. Linh had already called her, Tram looked at her watch and nodded, Linh still stood waiting her at the door. It was almost lunch time.

Linh put the untidy pile of papers on the desk aside to look at Tram:

-You had not have your lunch? Why do not you come in?

Tram said deliberately:

-As you are busy so I do not want to disturb.

-There is nothing important. Those men are from City Party Committee want to know about the current situation of our factory.

Linh sat down and went on to ask:

-Any thing you need me to help?

Tram took the empty chair that was next to the window and looked out the yard. It was baked sun, the hot air was evaporated on the tar road, the rose bushes along the fence was in full of green leaves without flowers, the row of eating houses on the other side of the road were crowded and noisy. The check point stand where policemen had checked people identification before they entered the city was exactly as before but there no more friends of the old days. Because of her silence, Linh started to ask again:

-It is the lunch time, if you agree we will go to have a lunch together as I do not bring any food today.

Tram nodded her head then following Linh to walk out.

After the lunch, Tram could not expect that Linh has gone to Ba Diem town with her to attend Phong's father funeral as she had allowed going home early today. Mr Huan's family was her old friend. Huan was an army major of former South Viet Nam forces before 1975, the chief of the 3rd bureau of Phuoc Long provincial military zone whose house was in front of the Nguyen Van Thoai public swimming pool. Phong was his first son who was the outstanding student of the famous Petrus Ky high school, passed the baccalaureate part two with high distinction grade but was not able to enrol into Sai Gon university because of his personal history as a son of 'people enemy' in the declaration paper issued by the ward administration office. Huan was imprisoned in the concentration camp as hundred thousand of the Southerners were and was taken to the North few days later. His wife had no choice. She quietly took her children to move to her mother's place in Ba Diem town. Their house was confiscated right at the first campaign of attack the comprador bourgeoisie of Ho Chi Minh city party committee. Tram brought Phong into the textile factory to be a process worker of the maintenance section after the day when she came to see his family. The last time when Mrs Huan went to the North camp seeing her husband was also the day Huan was released because his liver ulcer which had just almost killed him many times in this Lao Kay Yen Bai concentration camp in the virgin forest, far northern of North Viet Nam.

Being back to home not long, Huan had to move to Bu Dang new economic zone in Phuoc Long province, along the Kampuchea border, in obeying the tolerant policy of the new government. Mrs Huan has been poorly to take care of her ill husband since. At last, it was also not long Huan had died in a sorrowful morning rain as the torture of his liver ulcer. The village administration committee allowed her to take her husband's body to bury at the Ba Diem grave yard. Phong told Tram of the new in tears and asked for the permission to take few days off in her office, she held his hands sitting motionless in the corner. They had both sobbed without a word.

There were not many people at Huan's funeral. A couple of Phong's friends who were also workers of the factory just went home after their night shift, a few old men and women around , that was it, no drum, no clarinet, no song of calling up the soul. The cheap and broken wooden coffin was gradually lowered down to the grave in silence. Phong threw a couple of handful soil and few white tuberose branches over the coffin. He gazed it quietly, Mrs Huan and children wept softly for a long time. Her mother sat motionless against the foot of a tree. There was now no one in the grave yard. It seemed that all the ghosts had not come home yet to greet their new friend. Tram embraced Mrs Huan and her kids. She felt her lips were soaking in a sea of salt. Linh stood nearby gazing and said nothing, Linh turned her face away a couple of times. Over the field there still was the afternoon sun. Mrs Huan and her children went back home hand in hand. The tomb which was not taller than the thatch grass was being obscured behind. Mrs Huan thanked for Linh's presence at the funeral before she and Tram left. On the way to the highway, Tram's soul was in utter disarray. She could not know how Linh thought about it but she was pretty quiet all the way home. It was just dark enough when she left Linh's house. Man, her husband who went to do the private tutoring for children of few senior party cadres in Hai Ba Trung housing compound after school had not come back yet. The house was quite dark as ink.

After the funeral, Tram and Man had come to see Mrs Huan's family few more times but stopped a while. In deed they were really very busy to work for their lives. The living had now become harder, everything was more expensive but their salaries seemed to be nothing with a family of four members. However they determined not to give up the going. Tram used their saving to buy gold bars whenever she got enough money and hid them in a secret place in the house in case they need to use. In recent days, it was tumult in the textile factory as there were five or six workers of the despatching section had gone and arrived in Malaysia successfully. In the morning meetings Linh did not talk about this circumstance but she had once just asked Tram why they wanted to go. She avoided to use the word of 'betraying or to fawn upon the imperialists' as most of her communist party members did. Tram pretended not being interested in this kind of story whenever meeting Linh. The Factory party committee organised few urgent sessions to order all workers studying the policy of the government regarding the going and warned that whoever attempted to go illegally would be punished. Among those members of the committee, Mr Ba Bung, the secretary seemed to be the most reckless one who had loudest voice in fact he had just repeated exactly what his superiors said, more or less. Mr Ba Bung, a Northerner, who seemed not to be friendly with Linh although she was his manager. He stayed behind to carry out the communist underground activities in this city in many years so he considered that Linh knew nothing about Sai Gon city, he always said yes in front of her but tried to question her whenever he had a chance. He was also not happy when seeing Linh and Tram became close friends. He called Tram as a "puppet regime gangs". Tram was aware of that person but ignored him completely because they desperately needed her in the chief engineer's skills at least until this day. Like Man, her husband, she pretended ignorance, just did as being told, smiled at any body even they said black was white or yellow was red.

After the Tet, more prisoners had been released. Sai Gon was noisier than before. Ward and quarter policemen looked so busy all the time in putting those people under surveillance. Every prisoner had to report to the local police station weekly, even daily. The prisoners' families were not less busy than policemen. They had bustled up and down around Saigon city and other towns to look for the way of going. Again, the inmates had met each other in the strange streets. There was no more Duy Tan street with tall trees and dark shades. The cold cup of coffee sat lonely in a corner of the sidewalk which seemed to be bitter than the poisonous glass of Mr Phan Thanh Gian who determined to suicide instead of handing over the fatherland to the French colonial regime. Phong had not come to work in the last few days and had not come to collect his monthly salary. Tram was in doubt but felt happy if the thing would be right as she thought. The pay clerk had still kept Phong's salary come to see her asking what they would do. He was always nice and polite but anyhow he still was a local member of party committee thus Tram just asked him waiting for few more days.

On Sunday evening, the next ten days Phong had not come to the factory since, Tram and her husband went to visit an old friend, a former army officer of the South Viet Nam forces who had just been freed from Hoang Lien Son camp lived in a small alley next to Dac Lo high school. It was still early so they both decided to go to see Phong's family in Ba Diem. Mrs Huan let them know that Phong had gone with some other old friends from Long Xuyen province. His boat had arrived at Kijang island of Indonesia a couple of days ago. The whole family cried all day in joy. Tram and her husband had sighed with relief after getting this good news. They looked each other in tears. On the way home, Tram tried to find a good reason which would be as an answer for the administration board about Phong, particularly with Linh, anyhow it was Tram to offer him the job in this factory. Seven o'clock in the evening, dark cloud had slowly gone down over the horizon, Bay Hien passenger coach terminal was still busy with people got in and got off. Coaches to Tay Ninh, Duc Hoa Duc Hue towns were full of soldiers who carried their things from head to the foot.

Chapter Nine

Linh received a telegram from Ha Noi in late Friday evening. Her father was dead because of his lung cancer recurred in the last few months after being discharged from hospital. When he came to see her and Bon in Sai Gon, he looked so healthy and happier than the old days. He perhaps had seen the Sai Gon city in his naked eyes where uncle Ho Chi Minh left to look for a way to liberate Viet Nam and also where the Communist Party called it as an affected prosperous city during the wartime but every one of the Northerners still wanted to see this city at all cost even though they were poor peasants from a desolated country side or a party member from misty West lake of Ha Noi capital. On the day Linh's father came to Sai Gon by Thong Nhat express train, Bon was busy at the people city court so Linh went to Sai Gon train station by herself to meet him. Father and daughter who had seen each other for almost few years embraced each other in tears. Her father's tears were the tear of happiness. The dream of his life which he had always thought about at least came true at the days of his late life. Linh's father arrived in Sai Gon right at the Tet festival. Sai Gon streets was jubilant and animated every where in the Sai Gon people's hurry lives. His heart was in a boisterous brouhaha with the sound of fire-crackers and the petal of ochna flowers. They took him go to see a lot of interested places around Sai Gon without tiredness. He suddenly remembered a rainy night of July in more than thirty years ago when over- hearing Sai Gon radio which was still around his soul. That night, the broadcaster took the Sai Gon feelings sending to the Ha Noi beloved girls through the song of La Do Muon Chieu (Wherever the Autumn leaves falling) which was written by Doan Chuan and Tu Linh, two northern song-writers before the 1945 revolution. The singer had killed his revolution heart broken in tears. He had secretly loved Sai Gon since that pouring night. Bon and Linh had not many friends, Huu, the Chairman of 5th district, Thanh, the deputy secretary of City Party Committee seemed to be busy in taking care of their new affairs who had rare chance to see Bon unless they had to ask him some favours. The cadres and officials of the tax and business departments had always avoided meeting Bon but in general speaking Bon realised that they were really happier and richer than his family, even the policeman of the ward where Bon lived also had a new Honda motorbike and spent a lot of times in coffee shops or restaurants. Anyone could see that clearly, not only Bon but where the Party was, where the uncle Ho Chi Minh words. Bon sometimes felt sick of this happening but still believed on one dreaming day.

Linh wanted to talk with Bon about taking her father to visit Tram's place, Bon was hesitant at first but let his wife to decide it later on. They had not prepared yet, Linh met Tram and her two girls by chance in front of Ban Co market in the sunny noon when taking her father to go to buy few things before he came back to Ha Noi. Girls both bowed low to greet them, Tram said in happy voice at once:

Before you come back to Ha Noi, I like to invite you come over my place to have a family dinner.

Linh's father seemed to worry as looking at Linh for help. Tram did not wait for their answers, said:

-Please do not worry, just treat us as your children, we are close friends.

Linh said this time with a soft voice:

-I intent to take him to see you one day too before he leave Sai Gon, fortunately we meet you here

Tram repeated her invitation once again:

-Linh and also Bon do not forget to take your father to my home this evening, we will have a dinner altogether.

Linh nodded with a smile, Tram told the girls to say good bye with low bows, Linh held her father's hands to walk across the street, her father turned his head to look back. Tram looked her children with a vague smile then turned back to inside the market building to buy some more vegetables. It seemed to be rain soon, the baked sun stopped a while ago and there were a few patch of black cloud over the top of the Duc Ba cathedral. Today was the 5th day of the Tet.

On the day he went back to Ha Noi on the Express

train Ha Noi-Sai Gon, Tram and her husband came to see him off at Sai Gon station. He held Man's hands emotionally to say thank him for his gift, few boxes of very good Korean Ginseng and an expensive wool jumper that was sent from one of Tram's friend in Canada who left Viet Nam on April 30th 1975 on a merchant ship. He admired the good heart of Sai Gon people, the Sai Gon city where he had loved in silence from the night he over-listened the Sai Gon radio. Bon and Linh also bought few things which would be gifts for some friends over there. They could not believe the good bye of that time was the last time they saw each other.

Hung, a military doctor of the former South Viet Nam forces who was still allowed to keep the job at Binh Dan hospital offered the couple two air-tickets to Ha Noi when receiving the sad news. Bon had helped Hung settling the dispute of his grandfather's house that had been seized by the Ward Administration Committee. With these air-tickets Linh was back to Ha Noi right at that evening after. Her father's corpse was taken home by her aunty who lived in Ha Dong town. The sole coffin lay lonely in the middle of the old brick house without the smell of white paint although it was now in the days of Tet. Early spring, Ha Noi was in the season of apricot flowers. It was still glacial and misting over the tottering streets, also a few fine rains. The desolated house was still the desolated house, there was no visitor since Linh had left. Her late father lived alone till the last day of his life. Luckily there still were the smell of incense and the candle lights in the room, if none his death was only a meaningless cold corpse before the fall of South Viet Nam. Linh cried a lot at first but kept silent afterward.

Quietly they took the coffin to a sad grave yard in the outskirt of Ha Noi city on a very old funeral coach passing Co Ngu street in order to let him have a chance to see the Turtle Tower in Returning Sword Lake the last time before being buried deep down in the indifferent earth. After the funeral, Linh left the house for her aunty taking care of. They came back to Saigon on the next day. In Linh's mind, the Ha Noi of 36 streets was only a little thing to remember.

Motionlessly, Tram stood to gaze to those workers who were putting all default rolls of material aside in the despatching area and the machine at the entry door where Phong often wondered around on the first days he had just started his job in the factory. Suddenly she felt sad boundless, Phong had already gone almost ten months. She thought idly that when it would be her turn. When seeing Phong's mother, Mrs Huan who sold the apricot blossoms at Ba Chieu market on the evening of the December 30th, Tram was told Phong had entered the Malaysian Red Cross refugee camps and would be interviewed by American delegations soon. Mrs Huan said in full smile, this smile seemed to be fresher than all petals of apricot blossoms which were on sale. Tram did not hide her intention of going when she was aksed about her family plan in the near future. When leaving the market, Mrs Huan offered Tram a thin branch that full of bright yellow apricot blossoms as a good luck wish of the Tet.

Chapter Ten

The Vietnamese Communist forces pushed their men crossing the Kampuchea border in supporting a break away group of Khmer Rouge which was fighting against Pol Pot regime entering Phnom Penh capital city. All the Vietnamese youth were mobilized nationwide to carry out the military services. At this time, children of all families who were officials and army officers of former South Viet Nam government were named on the top of the list, especially those who were still in the concentration camps. The central government called upon people to take part in the fight against Pol Pot of Kampuchea on radio, television, newspapers daily but without a word about those who had not returned to their villages or how many men had died in the battle. Sai Gon suddenly was noisy as a wave of fever, from the top of the alley down to the end of the street, people talked about how to bribe the local authorities to avoid this death mission everywhere including how much they have to pay to get their relatives being out of the concentration camps before it was too late to go. There were a lot of people who had escaped successfully but there also were plenty of Communist Party cadres became richer. The policemen erected more check-points in the city to examine all the men but there were not many among them were arrested. The youth, boys or girls, were still crowded at cinemas, public gardens, restaurants in streets of Sai Gon.

In the middle of summer, it was not pouring down in Sai Gon, just a few fine rains in the morning. Streets were full of dust in scorching sun days. Flamboyant flowers were opening throughout the end of the way home, from the yard of Trung Vuong high school to the gate of Gia Long high school while listening to the bell of Xa Loi pagoda stroke. Here, markets were still crowded as before 1975 but there were less the buyers than beggars who asked for a pity Dong or a last drop of a soup of a beef noodle bowl which was left by the rich communist cadres in the restaurants. Somewhere in a corner of the street, the disabled soldier in a ragged marine uniform, even had lost one of his arm, had still tried to play a broken song with his old wooden guitar in hoping to have a few mercy Dong. There seemed to be a few coins in the worn cotton hat on the ground, he looked down and swallowed his salty tears which had just burst out the edges of his eyes.

The policeman with a cold and thin face stood to gaze him a while then moved toward the disabled soldier but he stopped at half way and walked away without looking back. Nearby, in Nam Duong cafe on Trieu Da street, cigarette smokes and the smell of coffee mixed together like morning dew from early dawn. Night dew had not yet disappeared on the bush of night lady flower in the quiet villa nearby where there was a military jeep and a soldier who carried his submachine gun to wait. A group of children without shirts gathered around a heap of rubbish at the end of the wall began to fight each other to take each single one of dirty and black plastic bags despite the stink smell.

The government had followed the step of Russian, its big comrade to launch the policy of economic reform, The Party general secretary, Nguyen Van Linh, on behalf of the Communist Party allowed people to set up private business as a form of limited free market and encouraged them to speak up and critic the government policies and the working attitudes and ways of their cadres or officials from wards, hamlets to districts, provinces even the central government. It seemed that Nguyen Van Linh wrote few articles in government control newspapers regarding the bribe and the corruption nationally. Taking advantage of this rare occasion, everywhere restaurants, general stores, food stalls so on were set up as mushroom field. Here was the clothing factories, over there was the export companies. Televisions, refrigerators, motorbikes and cars began to be seen in almost all big cities. However people would not get any approval from the City Administration committee without the patrons who often were senior cadres of the city authorities directly or indirectly. The centre bank of government had also involved in this opportunity in lending business loan in return to have its shares of profit. Policemen would ignore street vendors those were selling or buying daily goods provided they had some things but if whoever set up a big business as import, export foreign made things companies would be in big trouble if they had not have the connection with government agents, they had to remember to declare the name of Vo Van Kiet or Phan Van Khai in their applications. Cabarets, dancing clubs were allowed to be re-opened where men of the new red capitalist class had a place to spend their bribed money all night long and where they could listen to the loving songs and preferred to drink USA beer legally. They had enjoyed abandoning two words of "communist party" outside the doorsteps easily before stepping into the luxury hall to satisfy their night with beautiful girls and excellent western wines.

Unluckily, low ranking soldiers who had no power, no money had resigned to wander in the streets astoundingly, counting their steps in the middle of the baked sun in the city which was named Ho Chi Minh gloriously. They looked at the policeman in sweet-smelling uniform who sat to drink a glass of cool and icy milk coffee inside the restaurant then swallowing their own dry saliva painfully waiting for the soldier's ration next month which would be sold in the market somewhere although it was only enough to buy a few kilos of rice.

This day, in Sai Gon there were more people than before. Streets were always crowded. They fled the new economic zones in Binh Duong, Song Be areas to flock into Sai Gon. They came from the North who did not want to be back to Ha Noi. Gradually people now used to talk about money or US dollar more than the law, thus the domination of city government seemed to run away somewhere. Free market was the first priority, the top story of all. The love of communist party suddenly became the second thought. A lot more prisoners were freed to be back home day by day, those who were considered as the most dangerous enemies had already died in virgin forest without a word. Those who opposed the Party had gone and arrived in Malaysia, Thai Land, Indonesia luckily. No one wanted to stay if being asked as said once if the street lamp post could walk it had gone long time ago. The city party committee members had been changed few times in recently, the political executive bureau where Bon was the bureau chief was disbanded. In carrying out the central order from Ha Noi, the city party committee decided to emerge this bureau into the Party ideology bureau which was under the City Chairman's authority. Bon who had always worshipped his communist party ideology that ran throughout his blood and like his godfather, Bon dreamt to sacrifice for the nation and the party forever and he was proud of his clean life of a loyal party member. Thus Bon was neither this wing nor the other politically so no one seemed to like him. On the contrary, Huu, the Secretary of 5th district, the richest district of Ho Chi Minh city, was with the current top leaders of the city committee. Bon lose his position and was appointed as the section deputy chief of the bureau of party history research, a position that no one wanted to take it. Bon wrote a letter to his godfather in Ha Noi telling him his situation but received no reply. Bon quietly walked to his office twice a day in the broad daylight of Sai Gon streets. The old army Russian jeep was returned to the city authority right at the day Bon's office which was behind the city theatre was closed. It now became a luxury restaurant of a Taiwanese. In Sai Gon, the autumn had just come, fallen leaves covered full of both two street sides, few fine rains, it was so sad like an end of autumn day when Bon left

Ha Noi for Moscow, the day that Bon's heart was full of joys in the sound of the military music "this autumn, the 23rd day we went to the battle for the call of liberation of our motherland" of the old revolutionary days years ago. Bon stood alone in a quiet corner of the street to look up those dead tamarind leaves fell loosely with the evening wind. In Bon's heart, this day, there was no more "the 23 rd day of autumn".

In Friday evening, after school, Man went to pick Tram up at Vinatexco factory then headed to Phu Lam quarter where they would talk with one of their old friends about the escape. It was the end of autumn. There were still some full red bougainvilleas on the fence of factory. The guard had just opened the heavy gate, Tram walked toward Man from the building hastily and looking back to say something to Linh. Man waved his hand, Linh waved back with a smile. On the way to Phu Lam, Tram told her husband about Bon's situation, Man did not ask further.

Chapter Eleven

The Thong Nhat express train arrived at Ha Noi central station quietly after a long and weary night. It was very glacial in the morning, streets were dived in the thick mist of the mid-winter days, few thin men had scattered thinly walking back and forth as the shadows of sorrow night ghosts in Chinese fairy tales. Bon put the carrying cotton bag on shoulders, elbowed other passengers who almost were vendors from the South out to get off the train. There were a number of people stood around a tea-stall on the kerb of the end of a quiet street. The wood-fire next to a foot of an old dying Malabar almond tree which was set in early that night was still smoked. In the severe cold, Bon elbowed the crowd out to step in to buy a hot bowl of dark tea, drank it in hurry and pulled the collar of his Nam Dinh khaki shirt up to his chin to walk fast toward the Bach Mai hospital.

On the day when receiving the new of his godfather's death which was informed by his superior, Bon had packed a few belonging things in silence to go back to Ha Noi for the mourning. In the end, Bon's godfather had gone in his loneliness, the loneliness of the dream and his life. The Party had done him a favour at least, they granted him, a faithful servant of the communist party, a former minister of the Revolutionary Provisional Government of South Viet Nam, the agent of the North which was disbanded right as soon as the red and yellow star flag rising over all the Southern cities, a humble lot of land in a desolated grave yard in Ha Noi suburb.

It was just noon Bon arrived at the hospital, his godfather's corpse which was covered under a faded white sheet lay in the middle of a dark and stink room lonely. Bon was the only close relative beside the bony dead body that seemed to be smaller than the coffin size without the top. They supposed to give the hospital staff the permission to bury him yesterday but this was delayed as there was no truck available so Bon had not missed his chance to see him luckily. Bon had pity on him and on his harsh life. His family, his ex-wife and own children who had lived without his care did not care a thing of him, his days were the devoted days for the dream of gloral revolution of the Communist party, the days of liberation of South Viet Nam. He walked away from his family in the light of the oath to be at uncle Ho and party service despite his wife who had raised the children in the harsh life.

In the days before the liberation, when being in Sai Gon city, Bon sometimes came to his family's place in hoping to have a chance to see them and let them know that he was still alive but they left Viet Nam on 29th of April with the wave of fled people like the wave of northerners who left Ha Noi to go to the South almost 20 years ago after the Geneva accord was signed. Bon was back to Ha Noi to let him know the new, he kept quiet over few days without a word, that was why he had not wanted to come back to Sai Gon since even the war was over and his dream of liberation of the South was completed.

In that evening, with the help of a few hospital staffs and the fat female doctor who looked exactly like a female soldier in the Truong Son mountain campaign, a Molotova truck was arranged to take the coffin to the grave yard. Hastily, the grave was brought down into the earth without Catholic priest, without Buddhist monk. There was no sound of prayer, no smell of traditional incense. Bon sat and cried alone in front of the newly grave. There was a mixed sound of the evening wind and the bell of a pagoda at a far distance. Bon stood still in quiet trying to remember where the grave was in his mind but he wondered when he would be back this place. Lingering in Ha Noi, Bon tried to see a couple of old friends in hurry then going back to Sai Gon the following day. Falling Malabar almond leaves dropped on the way to Ha Noi train station. It was late evening, some kids had still set the dead leaves on fire. The train whistle had rent his heart and tears ran down on his face. Bon looked back at a far distance behind where there was a man's lonely grave that had more self-pities and shames than glories in his whole life.

Once again, the city authority celebrated their victory of the liberation of the South. SaiGon streets were full of red flags and political banners, a group of political bureau member who was on behalf of the Party arriving in Sai Gon to preside the event. They sat imposingly on the first row of the stand which was erected in the front yard of the former South Viet Nam president palace to listen the city committee members reading the reports of their success of last year work without a word of failure. Indeed, they needed not to build any thing because all what they wanted such as properties, housing, rices and money of the South were confiscated and belong to the Party long time ago as expected. Policemen had peace in mind to do their jobs money was often full in the pocket. Bicycles were only used by the low ranking soldiers this day. The policeman had already have Honda motorbike more than years ago at least. Some officials of former South Vietnamese government had gone to take refuge abroad, the rest who were accused as 'the people's enemy' were still imprisoned in dark and virgin forests over the China border would be dead soon or late. The City Chairman who had both read his speech and looked his polished Mercedes car and the driver who stood waiting in the car park ended the speech with a satisfying smile. Standing next to the foot of a tree in the public park, Bon looked toward the stand indifferently where just two years ago he sat and enjoyed the people's applaud whenever the speakers ended their speeches. Bon shook his head wearily and walked back to the market quarter quietly. The tamarin leaves fell as a curtain of fine dust on Le Thanh Ton street in the midday. At a corner of the back street of Ben Thanh market, a policeman who was sitting on a Honda talked to a couple of flea-market girls with a loud laugh. He seemed to be proud of his manner.

Bon lowered his head to speed up toward the bus stop at the beginning of Pham Hong Thai roundabout. Sai Gon was almost being in midday break. The fade red flag on the top of Sai Gon train station roof was not yet replaced although today was the celebration day of the great spring victory April 30th 1975.

Chapter Twelve

After Phong left, there were few more workers who had also gone successfully, some were in Malaysia, others were in Indonesia and some arrived in Canada, France, America or England as political refugees. At the time Phong had gone, no one dared to talk about that in this factory except few accused word of the party committee members but recently, the escaping stories became a normal and common so every one talked about it again as much as they liked. Even the Party secretary committee had given up. Workers paid no attention on the threat of city authority at all. Looking around, the whole nation, from Hai Phong of the north to Ca Mau of the south, nearly two thousand kilometres apart tried to go. Those who stood at the corner of street or the end of the alley often talked about the going rather than the staying if they had a chance. Communist cadres were busy to look for the fast way to make money for their own so no one showed any interesting in listening of that kind of story which every body had already known since the fall of South Viet Nam.

Tram walked up and down along the way between two rows of weaver machines, it was the lunch time, the sound of machines that ran slowly and tiredly in the hot temperature of early summer days made her felt so sad for herself. She was not hungry so she walked around the repairing quarter then stepped out the cement yard instead of going to Linh's office. Wasted chemical liquid which ran down to Tham Luong creek from the textile factory was smelt too stink at a far distance although it was no wind. The flamboyant tree lines on the other roadside were in full red blossom season. Once more, another summer came, she sorrowful counted it secretly she had already waited a number of summers, she shook her head wearily to walk back to her office through the workers' car park. Outside, it was full of sun.

Passing by Linh's office, the door was opened, Tram walked slowly and turned to look inside, Linh sat to gaze some things on the desk intentionally. Tram knocked gently, Linh looked up, Tram asked with a soft voice:

-Have you had some things to eat?

Linh had both answered and made a gesture to invite her coming in:

-I do not feel hungry today besides there still are some works to be completed so I am not keen to go.

Tram sat down on the chair that was next to the window looking out the yard as usual. Linh picked those untidy papers up in hurry to put them into the draw, her acts looked not so comfortable as usual. Tram pretended not to be aware of Linh, she walked toward and sat next to Tram. Both of them had just gazed over the busy road in silence. After a while Tram started the talk:

-Any things I can do for you?

Linh kept quiet a moment:

-I will go home early today perhaps!

Linh had not waited for Tram to continue, she said:

-This Saturday evening, do you plan to do any thing, I like to invite you to come to our place and we will have a dinner together, you, Man and the girls.

Tram was so surprised to accept her invitation. The clock on the wall said two o'clock already, Tram stood up to walk toward the door, Linh followed her behind a short distance before Tram turned to the way to her office.

Linh lost her job as the state-own Vinatexco textile factory. It was replaced by a senior party member of the ministry of internal commercial from Ha Noi. The car which Linh has used daily now also had a new boss. The poor workers of this factory did not bother who the new manager was. Just twice a day coming and going to the factory like the high tide, low tide of Sai Gon river. The Factory party committee members looked noisier than before, Mr Binh, the new manager who spoke with a pure Northerner accent rarely sat in his office. He had been seen to stand at the entry way of the main building, looking up and down without a word even an easy nod. He went to Tram's office to ask her a lot of questions about her skills with the secretary of the factory party committee and the section secretary of union who were always next to the manager wherever and whenever he went. This had not happened in days when Linh was still on that position. The morning meeting was lasted longer than before and they added a self-criticising part on the agenda. Tram had already not felt easy to work with them even the workers who talked less and smiled less than few months ago. They all tried to avoid meeting with them. Since Linh had not been here any more, whenever passing the manager's office, Tram suddenly felt there were some sad things deep in her heart that was very hard to be described by a single word.

It was almost a month, after the day Vinatexco factory had new management board. Some of section leaders were sacked or were lowered to a lower rank. There was no word about Tram but she was feeling that her days would come around the corner soon.

End of the summer, it was cloudy hastily although schools had just re-opened a couple of days. It was not rain yet but Sai Gon had started to be cold. Over Sai Gon river there were morning fine fog somewhere. Tram had not seen Linh again for long time since the day Linh had left Vinatexco. Tram and her husband passed by her house on Phan Thanh Gian street which was renamed Dien Bien Phu street some times, the metal gate was still opened as it was, they really did not want to enter because they did not know what to say. Man continued to keep his job as a teacher as usual. His cousin's family who owned a book shop in the corner of Tran Quy Cap street, next to Nam Quang cinema, whom they had just seen two weeks ago now had arrived in Jakarta. Now the book shop was the office of The National Fatherland Front. Both of them sat in a daze in dinners in next following days without a word despite their innocent girls ran and played all day long as usual. The girls did not mind what their parents thought. They still loved to go school every morning while did not forget to have a red scarf around their white blouse collars. Looking at her children Tram had heart broken. Just such age of life they had already carried the communist cangues on their necks.

Friday afternoon, Mr Ba Bung, the secretary of Factory party committee returned the self-criticism paper to Tram and demanded her to re-write it because it was not good enough in term of the requirement of party. She did not care as she realised that it would be her turn. She talked it over to her husband. Man was not against her decision of resignation. The following Monday morning, she arrived at the factory very early to put her resignation on the manager's desk joyfully instead of the monthly self-criticism paper. She went around the main building before walking in her office. It was full sun on the yard, she took her belongings, looked at the uncle Ho Chi Minh photo on the wall the last time, in her heart a freedom land appeared over the open sea. The manager was very happy to approve her request at once without a question then asked her to hand over her office right at that afternoon. Standing to wait for the coach to the city on other roadside, Tram looked into the vast cement yard where there were still few sun-rays of the end of the day. A few sparrows flew up and down over the old power lines. Gently, Tram had just touched her hair that ran down to the shoulders and smiled with herself like the smile of a bird that was set free out of the cage.

Chapter Thirteen

Bon and his wife moved into a small timber house in a tiny alley of Nguyen Thien Thuat street, not far from the Nguyen Thien Thuat housing compound. The villa on Phan Thanh Gian street was handed back to the city authority on the day Linh lost her job. They did not bring along any valuable thing, except the bed, two old wardrobes, a couple of chairs and few pots, few bowls, some cutleries. That was it. Her female servant came back to her village in Sa Dec province. The villa now was occupied by The Chief of city planning committee who was a Chairman of Ho Chi Minh City Administration Committee's cousin. Bon went on with his work of study the history of Viet Nam Communist Party which his comrade did not want to talk of this day. Standing at the bus stop sometimes, Bon seemed to be desperate to see Sai Gon people and including his comrade enjoyed to amuse themselves. The materialist side in his party now seemed to be more than the idealist. The party did not need asking Bon to write the end of the year report. Most of the reports of other departments were full of the word of money. Linh now was transferred to the City Education department being in charge of the training of primary teacher, she also rode the bike to work as her husband did, from one school to another talking about the conscience of a good teacher, however the more lessons she talked the more teachers left their jobs. Being a bicycle repairing man or selling goods in the flea market had still made more money than teacher's starvation wage. The social class order of Scholar, Farmer, Worker and Soldier was now turned upside down. Linh wanted to come back to Ha Noi sometimes but there was no one known over there. Perhaps just a little fine dust on the way home after school of the young age in old days. Back to Ha Noi in waiting for few sudden rains which made someone's heart broken in the misery of life. Bon now talked less than before as his word only was meaningless thing. No one wanted to talk about the anti-America involvement, even the Communist party members although they sacrificed at least nearly ten million men for the war in twenty years or so. Except his wife, Linh, Bon had not had any one else, there was no word of his parents since the days he had left Sai Gon. His foster parents, Mr and Mrs Nhan brought with them their resentment into the grave forever.

Sunday evening, just arriving at home from My Tho after taking her two girls to go to see their grandmother Mrs Huan had come at her place. The two women were absorbed in the talking as they had seen each other for a long time. Mrs Huan this time, let Tram know that her second girl, Phong's younger sister had gone who was being in the Galang island of Indonesia, she would take her youngest girl to go soon. She came to say good bye to Tram's family as she would not know if they would still have a chance to see each other again. She also introduced to Tram a trusty group which was dealing with the going. After Mrs Huan left, Tram and her husband were awake until midnight Suddenly it poured down in the middle of the night, there were a lot of laughing in the building on the other side of the street where the cadres of the city administration committee lived and the light inside though it was almost early morning.

Once again, party members of the city committee got ready to be changed. The state-owned newspapers started to run a number of articles of corruptions and bribes inside their organisation. They named a couple of high senior members with full of evidences of taking bribes, abusing their power to do unlawful business with private export companies to fill their pockets. Sai Gon people pretended not to see and hear anything, they did not care who would be changed or would be promoted. It was still sunny and rainy in Sai Gon city, markets were also busier than before, the Northerners tried to buy any thing even those goods were sold with a dear price. A lot of high cadres were charged of corruption and bribery but party members of Ho Chi Minh city party committee in turn drove new imported car from Japan. Poor people still went on to ride Chinese bicycles from this generation to the other. There were no more reading newspaper sessions in the quarter or the ward nightly. Local policemen who seemed to have plenty of spare time, liked to sit in the cafe rather than in their offices. The ruling party seized more vacant houses as their owners had gone more than previous days. Ward offices and party offices, one by one, were moved amazingly in to new premises. They did not bother to leave the old offices to the lower ranking officials. Sai Gon was still called Sai Gon despite communist flags and red propaganda banners erected over the city, not Ho Chi Minh city, even the policeman who stood in the check-point at the gate into the city from surrounding provinces or the female soldier who was busy with her heavy pack of goods to wait for getting on the coach preferred to call two lovely words "Sai Gon".

After the moon festival, Mrs Huan and her little girl left Viet Nam safely, the Tram's family planned to go with them on the same trip but they were still shorted some gold bars to pay unfortunately so they had to wait for next boat. The man who was the leader of the group came to Tram's house letting them know that Mrs Huan and her little girl arrived in Malaysia successfully although their boat was in the rough sea some days. He asked Tram to be prepared for the next one, about a month time. The following days, after school, Man went around some flea markets, from An Dong market to Kim Bien market or Ham Nghi old quarter to look for some needed things for their trip. An old friend, a military doctor of former South Viet Nam regime who had still worked in a medical station of Chi Hoa ward gave them some. This doctor had also been waiting his parting day with another boat in Can Tho area.

Tram's uncle, the retired army colonel whom Bon helped to be released earlier from Day Giay concentration camp had died. He was buried in 18th road cemetery in the border of Phu Tho Hoa village. Tram's mother came to give a hand from My Tho in organising the funeral. She stayed back with them few more days instead of going back to My Tho right away. On the parting day her eyes was still in tears. Ha, her uncle's eldest daughter hold Tram's mother to sob on Phu Lam coach terminal, her younger sisters stood beside Tram also cried unstoppable. Man stood motionless on the street side turned his face away in trying to hide his tears streaming down. Over his mother-in-law's shoulders the evening sun was setting.

Chapter Fourteen

Sai Gon had just been in early winter days, there were not many rains, just a few fine one. It was sunny in the streets but not scorching sun like middle summer days however it had just brought a few warm minutes for those who walked up and down in the deserted alley. The two sisters walked up and down inside the building of Ban Co market a while then left there to go to a sugar-cane juice stall on the other side of Phan Dinh Phung street. Tram had just taken the glass from the sale girl. Also Linh had just stopped her bike at the kerb. Tram was so surprised while holding the glass in her hand. Linh nodded with a half smile. It was a long time the two had seen each other since the day Linh had moved out of the villa on Phan Thanh Gian street. Tram and her husband passed that villa sometimes but not stopped by while seeing some strangers. Ha said hello to Linh and walked back to the market again. Ha had gone, Tram asked Linh to move close to the tree shade next the stall. Just a few words Ha had already come back from there with a few small paper bags. It was just over midday, Tram invited Linh to have some things for lunch in a noodle restaurant nearby but Linh had declined with a soft voice. She gave Tram her new address then pushing the bike down the road. Tram held the paper in hand to say good bye, Linh was gradually obscured in the middle of the crowded streets. The two sisters said no word.

End of August, Mr Huu, the Chairman of 5th district was arrested by the City police department at his home. The rich property which he gained without tears and sweats in few short years was temporary confiscated pending to the court order. The City Police weekly magazine had printed the new of that arrest and accused Huu has abused his power to manipulate the banking lending rules, to deal illegally with private sector in fraudulent and taking bribes. His total amount of money was up to billions Dong. No one in this 5th district was surprised about the new, every one knew Huu had a lot of shares in many private companies around the 5th district especially in Hoang Huy clothing factory which was approved a license to export and employed more than five hundred workers, behind the Sung Chinh hospital. The economic policemen and tax officials raided and searched and closed Hoang Huy factory two days before Huu had been arrested. Huu's family moved to his wife's mother place at the end of Hong Bang street which she was the owner, this house was belong to a high ranking army officer of the former South Viet Nam regime who was released earlier from Moc Hoa prison after his wife had a talk with Huu's wife few weeks ago. Not long after going back home, no body had seen this family in the house any more. They saw Huu's driver came there sometimes with Huu's wife then her mother moved in. A number of officials and party cadres were arrested afterward but the state did not say what the charge was, however according to the state owned media this day, including the Ho Chi Minh city youth magazine, they were charged of corruption. Huu and those people were put in Chi Hoa prison to wait for the day to be put on trial. Their families were not allowed to visit them. A new chairman had come to replace Huu in 5th district. The Chairman's villa was repainted and renovated as the Chairman suggested from the fence to the steps, it looked quite different with the old one. The swimming pool in the back yard seemed to be larger than before. The Kim Bien flea market was busier than the old days, the forbidden songs, love song, not the military songs, were played loudly in the row of cafe on the street side along the market quarter. There was a huge crowd of policemen, officials, party cadres and party members who were in and out all the time despite early misty morning or dark night. Traffickers felt easy and free to do their business in front of policemen who always turned their faces away while filling their uniforms pockets. The public garden which was next to the 5th people administration committee office, opposite Chu Van An high school was not too large where all sort of girls, almost prostitutes gathered around, some stood up, some sat down. There were also a lot of soldiers in Nam Dinh khaki shirts hid behind some dark bushes from early dawn.

Saturday evening, after leaving her cousin who lived

next to Tam Tong Mieu pagoda on Cao Thang street where it was next to Nguyen Thien Thuat housing compound, Tram decided to stop by Linh's home to see them as she was to be going in about few days. Linh was at home alone, Bon had gone somewhere since early afternoon. Tram sat on the chair next to the window to look around inside. There were a couple of aged furniture and a couple of pictures of Ha Noi and Moscow and wild flower were hung up unevenly on the fade white wall. Linh poured the hot tea out of a blue Chinese made thermos bottle into a white cup and handed it to Tram:

-Why do not you let me know in advance you will come! Sorry the house is in a mess.

Tram took the cup and smiled gently:

-We are sisters so need not to do so, as on the way home from my sister who lived close here, I just stop by.

Tram asked Linh some normal things. Tram suddenly remembered Huu, the 5th Chairman who was arrested week ago and also was a friend of Bon, Tram looked at Linh:

-Do you know that Huu was arrested at home week ago? I think you and Bon may hear the report from police.

Linh looked so concerned:

-We know that new from some one who worked in my office, not from the report of police.

Tram had said anything yet, Linh went on:

-Huu is Bon's friend when the two were in same class in high school but not close until we were sent to the South, as you know, we met him few times in Sai Gon when he asks for Bon's help. He will not get away with his jail sentence. Whoever, if being jailed because of the charge of corruption or bribery will be certainly purged from the Party. He deserved what he did. He pays for what he did obviously but I am afraid of the situation where Huu will shift the guilt for his action on someone else. Bon has helped him sometimes so I just do care to ask if Bon is in trouble.

Linh poured some more tea into the cup in Tram's hand that seemed to be still full:

-Please have some more, thank you so much for your concern.

It was almost late. There still were few late sun-rays over the city. Tram pushed her bike into inside Linh's house. They walked to an open beef noddle stall at the top of the alley. The owner greeted them with a round smile. When leaving Linh's home, Tram promised to be with her again soon although Tram realised that there would not be the next time. This was the last and they would not have any thing to talk of. Tram asked Linh to say hello to Bon, Linh stood in front of the house to see Tram leaving, Tram had both rode the bike and looked back to wave her hand. Linh was not in hurry to go back inside.

That night, Tram was informed that their parting day would be within next two weeks when meeting with the leader, a middle age man, at Cay Sung street. Being so happy they needed not to take dinner and they could not believe that Ha, her cousin and her family would go in the same boat. Ha was really entrusting as she knew this group for a long time but she pretended to know no thing, saying no word until Man asked her about it month ago. It was late night. Man was not in hurry going to bed, just walked up and down in the lounge room with a happy face despite he had to go to school early tomorrow morning. Tram was in the same Man's situation. There was sound of vehicles moving from the Bay Hien intersection in the streets. The sun had just risen.

Chapter Fifteen

Taking few days off, Man and his wife took their two girls to My Tho city to see the grandmother and made careful recommendations of their house to her before leaving. A family with two siblings, Tram's eldest brother who was an Air born Force Captain of the former South Viet Nam regime was discharged from the military service after being wounded in the Ha Lao battle because of his disable left leg. After the fall of South Viet Nam in 1975 he came back to his home village to represent himself to the new local government as a low ranking soldier at the time the order given. As a soldier, he was not sent to concentration camp. Trieu, his only son who had not completed yet his fourth year of the Engineering Course in Phu Tho technical institute when Communist force took over Sai Gon. Quickly he jumped on a big merchant ship that was docking in Bach Dang quay left Sai Gon on early day of April 30th He and his wife had sighed with relief after getting the new of Trieu arriving in Philippine. Trieu was sponsored by a Uniting Church family and entered Chicago few months late. Trieu went to a technical college and had a job presently. Tram's brother and his wife now were living at their mother's place. His wife still had a teaching job at My Tho high school nearby. They also had a fruit stall in My Tho market so their living was still easy at least. Tram often went to see her family as the two cities was just only sixty kilometres apart. With her mind in peace, Tram felt totally assured to go.

Standing at the back veranda of the house to look out to the new bridge, My Tho river that flew along My Tho market was still very muddy and was in low tide and high tide twice a day. The row of house on stilts on the other river bank was old as it was before since the days she was a little girl. There still were few late flowers on the top of the cassia grandis tree line that stood along the edge of a big lake in the centre of the town although it was in the middle of winter. Tram had her heart wrung with pain at this scene to realise that she would not be here soon, she had not known that when she would be able to see her town again. She would not have a chance to stand at the sampan landing waiting for her schoolmate who lived on the other side of the river and she would also not have any more chance to stand at the roadside to look passionately at those red apricot fruits that sat nicely on open fruit stalls along the highway to Sai Gon at Trung Luong three crossway in the scorching summer days. She walked with her girls across the cement bridge. The two girls romped out to catch the afternoon light winds. Somewhere, at the end of the river, a couple of late evening sun-rays were falling.

In the morning, Ha had come very early when Tram prepared to take her daughters to school. They both walked with them and had a chat. Ha told her that Bon, Linh's husband was arrested yesterday afternoon. Her friend, the Chinese Vietnamese told her the new last night when she met him at a take-way food in An Dong market. Tram was so surprised and speechless in listening to this news. Tram did not dare to say that her judgement was quite right but among the corrupted communist cadres of this Ho Chi Minh city, she thought Bon and Linh were not bad at least. Any how they were her friends once and besides they had helped Tram's family a number of occasions, she could not stop to concern about Bon's fate so the two ladies rode the Honda slowly to pass Linh's house on Nguyen Thien Thuat street to have a look. The door was closed firmly and the house was quiet as usual. It was quite different with the scene at Huu's house few weeks ago where policemen surrounded the house from early morning until late night. They stopped and went in Hien Khanh cafe where they could look at the other side of the street. Streets were still crowded and noisy. People walked up and down hastily in the dusty sun of the midday. Suddenly thinking of the gold bars and all the gifts Tram made a slip of her tongue to say there was no reason why.

Bon was arrested because of details of the witnesses' declaration in Huu's court file regarding the period of time when Bon was the Chief of Political Executive Bureau. As police said, Bon had plotted with Huu to abuse their position and power taking bribe in a large of amount of money and released a lot of political prisoners from Pham Dang Luu central prison and former military officers and officials of the old regime. Although Bon's property was not confiscated at this time but state was in doubt that Bon could disperse and hide them when hearing of Huu's arrest. So while the investigation was processing, on behalf of the Party, Chairman of City party committee allowed Linh to stay at her present house. Linh also was allowed to visit Bon once a day. Each time was no more than thirty minutes. There was no one, no friend, even the Chief of section where Bon had worked and whoever had asked his help, tried to avoid meeting with Linh when she came to ask for help to clarify her husband's innocence that had shown his loyalty with the Party and sacrificed his life for the holy revolution of Vietnam communist party. A county court judge who was Bon's close friend declined to help although the two had shared with each other a piece of cold cooked rice, a tiny portion of salt in cold and raining days to cross Truong Son trails.

Linh took few days off to return to Ha Noi, the city where she thought she already forgot once. But now she was. Linh returned to Ha Noi to seek helps from the former Chairman of Ho Chi Minh city party committee who now a member of the central political bureau. Linh spent hours and days to wait for him in patience but at the end he had just refused with a callous smile. In the middle of winter, Ha Noi was glacial and freezing which seemed to cut her heart into pieces but it was nothing to compare with the cold in her soul. Linh wandered in Ha Noi streets as a homeless ghost in few whole days and came back to Sai Gon with her painful and broken heart.

The whistle of Thong Nhat train seemed to rent her life, her salty tears streamed down on her hatred face. There still were Malabar almond leaves falling on the way out of Ha Noi city and a few of spill of fire sat alone on the roadside to wait for the morning came somewhere over Hong Ha dike.

Chapter Sixteen

The director of Hoang Huy clothing import and export was sentenced to death. He was on the trial of corruption charge while Huu was still Chi Hoa jail. Some of city state bank officials who involved with this man to use fake documents in obtaining business loans and made a large amount of laundering money to Taipei and Hong Kong also were sentenced from 5 years to 15 year jails. They had no right to appeal. The factory was closed. Workers lost their jobs without pay. Both front gate and back door were under policemen's close watch. Sai Gon people seemed not to be interested on this matter in contrast they had just smiled secretly when reading the state owned daily newspapers. Those sentences would be carried out or not, it was only the Party or the state knew. There was no one else. Nationwide, from the North to the South every one knew Hoang Huy company very well where there were also the shares of the Chairman of Ho Chi Minh city people committee's wife, of the 7th Military corps General's wife and a lot of other senior party members. The state launched the anti-corruption campaign in the whole country, the Party Secretary General himself wrote few articles in newspapers to encourage people denounced and informed the authority but the guilty men who were used as the scapegoats were all low ranking cadres, people had not seen yet any of them who were on the top circle of the central government. Mr Huu and Bon continued to be in prison, a wretched prison life while no one knew that when they would be brought to the trial.

Once there was a moment, Tram was also affected to think of Bon and Linh, she really wanted to see them but this time, she also did not want to miss the decisive going again, the going which would decide their fates and was not easy to have in this difficult situation. It allowed her to make no other choice. Man, once again, applied for few days off to attend his late father's funeral. The female principal, a party member from Ha Tinh province, who often added the word "oh yes" to the end of her saying approved his request without hesitation with a smile as usual. Before the parting day, the group leader stopped by Tram's house to confirm the date and time. Tram's family had already packed up and was ready to go.

One day before the departure, Man went to Nancy market very early as arranged to be shown the spot where the sampan that people liked to call "a taxi" was and to recognise the steer-man. From here they would be taken through Sai Gon river to the big boat that was anchored in the mouth of the sea Vam Lang. The cafe was very crowded. Some was from countryside, the others from this city. It was sunny although the winter had just come a little early in this day. The steer-man, about thirty years old, who was very polite and honest taking Man to the sampan landing, at the end of Tran Binh Trong street, to show him his sampan and reminded Man what he had to do tomorrow morning. Half and hour late, Man and the steer-man went back to the cafe then left there in hurry. The sun rose higher over Sai Gon river. On the way home, Man stopped by his friend's home who worked in the same old high school before 1975. He now ran a book shop on Phan Thanh Gian street. Hoang, his younger brother, a special force lieutenant of the former South Viet Nam regime was shot by Communist guard right next to the fence of Thien Ngon concentration camp, northern of Tay Ninh city when he tried to escape with few other inmates in a pouring night. His family went to take his death body back home and burying him in Binh Chanh cemetery. They were also ready to go soon with another group. There still were a lot of people come and go in his book shop. As soon as Man came home Tram's mother had just arrived from My Tho. Ha's sisters and Tram's girls surrounded their grandmother to talk and laugh all the time. Ha rode the Honda with Tram to somewhere. Man stood at the front door to look back with a pleasant and full smile.

The boat which took hundred and fifty people including Tram's family had arrived safely in Indonesia after about six days or so in rough and open sea. Tram and her husband embraced their girls, their nieces to cry loudly when the boat landed on the sand beach, waves and waves in turn touched noisily. At the end of the horizon, behind the vast sea, Sai Gon was really lost in their eyes.

In Sai Gon, few weeks later, the group leader came to let Tram's mother know the good news. As Tram's arranged, she sold the house for the 18th Ward party secretary who lived and carried out underground activities of Viet Cong in Sai Gon as a nurse during the war time then returned to My Tho. She went to the Buddhist Pagoda in her home village to offer a pray for Tram's family. She was so happy in tears but she also cried to be afraid of the last day of her life. There was maybe no more change to see each other again.

Chapter Seventeen

On the day Tram's family arrived in Indonesia Mr Huu was sentenced to 25 years jail. State owned newspapers had just run the sentence without further comment. Ho Chi Minh city police department conducted Huu under escort to Hoang Lien Son prison, along the Chinese border on the military convoy which transported television sets, refrigerators and Honda motorbikes to Ha Noi city. His wife determined not to accompany her husband, she vowed to have better to be a "born in the North, died in the South" as she could not defy the seduction the "lipstick and face-power" of Sai Gon city in the past years. Life had been changed why she had to come back where she was once in days of "rain of the forest and wind of the mountain" of Lao Kai Yen Bai highland. Few visiting trips from the South were enough to repay for husband-wife relationship. She took To Huu's words, a famous communist poet's example, "to love the Party rather than her husband, to love Marxist-Leninist rather than her father".

Linh sat to sob her heart out alone in the dark corner of the room, the house was now more deserted than before especially since the day Bon had been put in jail. Linh thought that she would have a chance to save her husband when coming back to Ha Noi but she could not believed that the comradeship of many sacrificed years for uncle Ho and for the Communist party had become a completely empty word. Linh looked wearily around the house. White pain timber wall had faded through many seasons. The branch of yellow fabric made sun-flower in an old broken vase had become almost black and was covered totally under a thick spider-web. Linh sometimes wanted to be a Southerner in believing on the destiny but she did not want to give up her life, because until this moment, like Bon, they had still thought that their Party was till lucid. Linh had stood up slackly to look out through the front window, the sound of the children who played catch and run game on the yard of Nguyen Thien Thuat housing compound dragged out like the call of a ghost in the middle of a night fall. The cold rice bowl which had sat on the table since late noon had become dry and solid like a piece of stone salt. Nearby the sound of mosquitoes that had gone looking for its band were heard clearly. Standing against the wall, Linh kept crying, somewhere over the corner of the sky far away, it seemed to be raining although there still was no rain in Saigon this season. The policeman of street quarter rode the honda passing slowly and had a easy look at the house, Linh felt to be sad at heart.

Suddenly Linh had wished eagerly to see Tram again. It was long time Tram had not come to visit her, Linh wondered that she was aware of the new of Bon or not and if she had known that Linh now was in suffering situation. Since the date Bon had been jailed, Linh had not often come to her work place. The Manager of Ho Chi Minh education department who was a Southerner, from Go Cong province called her to his office few times, not for punishment but for counselling, he had comforted Linh and admonished her trying to ask some ways to save Bon. Listening what he said Linh felt her heart broken deeply. The fatherland's iron bulwark of the South that was named Ho Chi Minh had suddenly become too strange. It was stranger than Moscow city when she arrived there on the first day. Linh threw herself down on the ageing bed, closed her eyes in feeling a dark sky around the silence of this deserted house. There was a little light evening wind that blew slowly through the window, Linh dropped off to sleep a moment later.

In Sunday afternoon, on the way home after going to see Bon in Pham Dang Luu prison as usual, Linh stopped by a small flea-market at the corners of Le Van Duyet and Tran Quy Cap streets, next to Nam Quang cinema looking for some cough tablets in order to bring it to Bon tomorrow. Suddenly, Bon has had a severe cough in the last few days, his voice was not clear enough to be heard sometimes. She always cried whenever leaving the gate of the prison. She had to pull her palm-leaf conical hat down to cover her tears. All kind of vehicles had still flitted about in Saigon and the yellow star flags had gone on to fly brightly on every top of the tall buildings but there was no military music to be heard like on the first days when the communist forces marched into this city. Linh pushed her bike up to the kerb, a girl stood at a stall who gave Linh a sign of the price, Linh nodded her head to agree with. It was not far from here, two thin men who wore the old style of Northern costumes, the Nam Dinh bottle green khaki trousers and the old cotton helmets, the helmet which almost her senior comrades had thrown them in the corner of their wardrobes long time ago had carefully counted the notes to pay for a couple of new steel watches which they had just brought from a male street vendor. Linh put dozen of cough tablets into her hand bag and pushed the bike down on the street indifferently. The evening wind was still warm although it was now in the middle of autumn days. Linh rode her bike up to Phan Thanh Gian street trying to go to Ban Co market way. Linh met Mr Huu's wife who had walked out from a jewels shop nearby. Although she was not quite sure this was her but Linh had just nodded to greet so did Mr Huu's wife. Mr Huu's wife stopped waiting for Linh to put her bike against a foot of a big tree on the kerb. Once again, she greeted Linh:

-Hello Linh, it has been a long time.

Linh had just hung her hat on the handle of the bike and lifted her head up a little bit to respond:

-Hello sister Huu, are you still alright?

Mr Huu's wife shook her head:

-As same as you, we have nothing to say good or bad in this situation.

She stopped a little moment than went on:

-How is Bon, any hope?

Linh said wearily:

-I tried to beg some helps every where but.... it seems

to us that Bon has to go to the jail soon or late like Mr Huu.

When talking about Huu, Linh could not see any concerns or worries on his wife's face, she told her:

-We deserved what we did. Party was busy to take care of Party. Senior comrades take care of senior comrades. They have not enough time to fill up their pockets, no time left to have a pity on those scape-goats like us. Now we have to take care of ourselves, oh Linh.

Linh had a secret glance at Mr Huu's wife, from top to bottom. Her clothes were so expensive while she still wore all the old stuffs which had been used since the day she worked at Vinatexco factory. They talked to each other in few more moments than saying good bye. Before walking away, Mr Huu's wife gave Linh her address and an address of a friend of her who was now a high ranking official of the city justice department if Linh had any intention to seek help again. She also asked Linh to come to see her at home if Linh want to do so. Linh stood to look at her. She caught a cyclo that had just passed by. The image of Mr Huu's wife who walked out from a jewels shop at the entrance of Ban Co market had still haunted her on the way home.

Linh got hold of some things on the bottom of the wooden trunk in the corner of the room, she took a small paper packet out that was smaller than a fist and was wrapped by a dark yellow plastic bag. Holding the packet on hand, Linh sat on the chair, looked around if some one were seeing her although the door was closed and nobody else in this house. Gazing the shining golden gold bars that were reflected under the power light from the ceiling, Linh shredded in tears. All of a sudden, she thought of Tram's words when Tram offered her these gold bars, "do not let Bon know this matter, only you and me, just keep them in case you need to use them one day..". Linh held the packet against her chest and lay stretched out on the bed, letting her eyes closing in a little moment of joy. The night was already fallen long time ago, kids yelled out noisily in calling each other to go to watch television in the quarter leader's cafe over a section of the street. The sound of the wooden bell of the noodle street vendor that dragged out like a say of prayers was heard sorrowfully.

End of the summer, it started raining in Saigon. It poured down continuously in a couple of days. Streets were dived in snowy colour from Hang Xanh four ways crossing to Khanh Hoi area. Linh had still thought about going to see the relative of Mr Huu's wife and about the gold bars all the time since having met her at Ban Co market. Every time when coming to visit Bon, Linh wanted to talk to him about this matter but hesitating not to do so. Bon was weary and tiredly of his plight in this painful situation so he did not want to talk any thing. The only and last hope which this couple was trying to sponge on the lucid decision of the People Court where his friend was a principal judge and also was a close comrade whom Bon had shared with a piece of watery rice under the dug-out in the glacial rain of the Truong Son virgin mountain. Mr Huu had been conducted to the North more than a month. There still was no word from the Party committee. Linh went to the court trying to find out what was going on, they informed her that they were waiting the Party Committee Secretary's orders unfortunately. Now Linh could understand that, the

Party was the only one to make the ultimate decision on Bon's case despite of the existence of the City People Court. However the Party had really abandoned them since the day Linh had come back to Ha Noi looking for help. It would be in autumn in a next few days, thinking of the day when Bon would be conducted to the freezing highland forest of the North, Linh swept softly for a long time then deciding to use all the gold bars which Tram had given to her years ago.

Mr Huu's wife took Linh to see her cousin who was working in Ho Chi Minh justice department presently. The two ladies sat quietly in Givral restaurant looking out to the street, it had already passed ten o'clock in the morning, there still was not sunshine. Over the Saigon river, Bach Dang quay was entirely vague in the morning mist. People tried to cross the street hastily like the shadows of night ghost through the foggy glass windows where a couple of drops of mist dropped down as someone's tears. Suddenly Linh sighed depressingly to look the glass of coke on the table. Mr Huu's wife was still in joy as usual. It was not long the cousin of Mr Huu's wife had come in. Duan, was his name, at the same Mr Huu's age, who spoke the northern dialogue like Linh and seemed to be more courteously and effusively than a lot of other comrades in the government who Linh had met before. Linh talked less and letting Mr Huu's wife did the discussion. According his say, Mr Duan was a senior official of the central people's court of investigation who had been assigned to come to Saigon to work with the City Justice Department in relating those arrested people who were in jails currently. He would be back to Ha Noi in few days to report to the

Central Government his finding. Listening to his talk Linh secretly thanked Mr Huu's wife. When parting, he gave Linh some counselling and promised to help until the final bid. Linh stepped out the restaurant first left the two relatives walked behind. It seemed Saigon just had a few warm rays of sun somewhere.

On the day Mr Duan went back to Ha Noi, as arranged Linh had wrapped five bars of gold neatly in a piece of black paper then bringing it to him in reminding him to take care of her matter. Linh had not bothered to think that these gold bars would be lost or not. While Bon was still in jail the lost of these gold bars would be meaningless. Walking Linh to the door, Mr Duan gave to her his home address and his office address in Ha Noi and in the meantime he told her to come to see him in case if she would have a chance to come back to Ha Noi. Few days later, Linh came to Mr Huu's wife home to talk about Mr Duan especially asking her the reason not to ask him to help her husband. She let her know that Mr Huu's crime of embezzlement was too serious and they could not hide their properties, on the other hand Mr Huu had not shared equally among his superiors so even Mr Duan had hundred hands he could not do any thing about this. Her explanation had encouraged Linh to have a reason to hope. Even now if she lost every thing she had nothing to regret.

Schools had closed for summer vacation few days ago. The flamboyant flowers were opened in full on the streets in the scorching sun after heavy raining days. The mail man came earlier than usual who delivered an urgent telegram that was sent to Linh from Ha Noi. Linh opened the telegram hastily and trembled with excitement. Mr Duan said he had presented Bon's case to the Central People Court of Investigation and the Party Political bureau. He would let her know the result at once when he had their responses. After reading the telegram, it seemed that she had just smiled, a lonely smile which it seemed that she had not have once since a long time. Linh had still not told Bon about this when coming to see him in Pham Dang Luu prison during the following days. Mr Huu's wife stopped by to see Linh a couple of times but she always left in hurry, did not bother tasting the little dark and cold tea in the broken cup. Linh did not feel sad as at least she still thought of Linh. Twice a day, morning and afternoon, coming to the office and going back home, Saigon, the city where Linh and her husband had chosen to be home of the rest of their lives had become a cramped place of meaningless. The leafy and shady streets where all sort of vehicles flocked to come and go, where there were brouhaha of laughs and talks of their first days in the South were now only a sole way, from her home on Nguyen Thien Thuat street to Pham Dang Luu prison, the only known street was still present in her soul.

In Sunday evening, after leaving the prison, Linh rode the bike along Ky Dong street where there were a huge number of people, stood crowded to wait for the evening mass in the front yard of Chua Cuu The church. The vibrating sound of the bell make Linh lingered to go on. She covered her face while pushing the bike against the brick fences in a quiet corner. She stood motionless to look up the Jesus statue which was swallowed in the last evening sun-rays. Suddenly Linh cried out in tears when looking at every sign of the cross that had been made by the church-goers. On Monday of the beginning of the week, the court informed Linh that her husband's file would be heard within the next two days. She was panic in rushing to the central post office to make a phone call to Mr Duan who said to her that he had already knew this new but had not received yet any formally word from Comrade President of the Central People Court of Investigation. As a stunned woman, Linh staggered walking in the street, she repeated to herself the three words "it was too late". Linh crossed the street without any attention despite a police jeep moved passing by made a loud horn in warning. Linh stood alone at the middle gate of Duc Ba cathedral letting people come and go. She covered her face with the two bare hands, once again she talked to herself "Please help me my God".

Chapter Eighteen

Bon was stubborn to deny any wrongdoing and was still not willing to declare his hidden properties. After delivering Huu to the North, the city court gave Bon thirty years jail sentence and purged him out of the Party. Linh cried alone in the desolated house unstoppable in days, when uncle Ho died he brought with him the communist justice down to his tomb, the demagogic justice which Bon and Linh had worshipped and dreamt of all their lives. Linh sat motionless at the front of the city court, people was unruffled walked by indifferently. No one cared who and how she was. The policeman who guarded the building standing to give fresh loving smiles to a group of female street vendors on the other street side despite his boss was standing to wait for him at the gate. The horns of vehicles rented over the air as Thong

Nhat train whistle was when Linh left Ha Noi in feeling a cutting pain in her entrails.

Early morning, all sort of vehicles lined up on both side of the Pham Dang Luu prison where was more crowded than before but it seemed to be more equal, there were also all type of communist prisoners not only Sai Gon people. Policemen were armed with submachine gun AK-47 surrounded a very old ambulance vehicle. Its rear door was opened wide. It seemed to wait for some things. People tried to come closer in hoping to see what was going on. Not long after, a couple of policemen ran toward the ambulance vehicle in hurry then pushed the crowd off the main gate. The ambulance vehicle made a loud siren and was drove away to Bay Hien area.

Ho Chi Minh city police department was arranging to send Bon to the North as they did with Mr Huu. Yesterday, after coming to visit her husband as usual, Linh felt so desperately and was weary with this life on the way home. Linh sat to sob alone in the shadow of night. She hold a few gold bars tightly in her hand which had been returned from Mr Huu' s wife on behalf of Mr Duan who had apologised for having no power to save Bon this time. Linh felt headlong on the table and dropped off to sleep. There was still a known mosquito calling friends lonely around. In the damp cell of Pham Dang Luu prison at the same time, Bon sat lonely to look around, through the small square window, the power lamp of a street post radiated sallow light over the dark cell as a desolated cemetery on the last day of December. The light that Bon once had seen sparkling on the window grills looked the candle light on the top his godfather's coffin in Bach Mai hospital a year ago. Bon decided to end his own life by hanging himself with a dirty bed sheet. Bon brought with him the glory revolution of 23rd day of autumn of 1945 into the silent eternity at the midnight. In a water morning glory pond nearby, the deeply sad sounds of bull-frogs dragged out one by one. In the silence of night, it seemed the morning was still far away.

The doctor in charge of night shift who was waiting to be replaced put the stethoscope on the top of the bedside and shook his head as there was no thing else he could do. Bon's death body had become dark purple in the dim light of the mortuary. In the yard of Vi Dan hospital leaves were falling from the old flamboyant tree lines in the end of august of autumn.

In the evening, somewhere in a corner of the end of a street, one could see a thin and ruffed hair girl who was not a southerner sitting to feel lightly and for long a fade Nam Dinh khaki shirt on the sidewalk. She mumbled with herself like an insane women in the middle of the glorious city that was named Ho Chi Minh, the name that this girl once was dull to shout together "long live my dearest Uncle" and "long live the Communist Party".

Thuyen Huy was born in a poor village of Tay Ninh province in South Vietnam.

Graduate of National School of Pedagogy- Saigon.

Graduate of Saigon University (Arts) and National Institute of Administration - Saigon.

Being imprisoned in the re-education and concentration camp of Vietnamese communist regime after the fall of Republic of South Vietnam in April 1975.

Arrived in Australia as a political refugee in 1980.

Had Master of Education from University of Southern Queensland and Master of Education of Victoria University - Australia.

Living in Melbourne - Australia.

Worked as the writer and editor of a number of Vietnamese newspapers and magazines in Australia.

Teaching Vietnamese language at Victorian School of Languages - Melbourne - Australia.